EPHEMERA

SHORT FICTIONS AND ANOMALIES

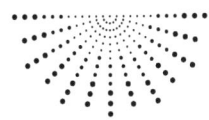

MICHAEL FERGUSON

CONTENTS

Foreword	vii
1. Choke, Gash, Umbra, Crispy and Carol	1
2. Murky Waters	13
3. Thorns	29
4. It Came From Outer Space and Wouldn't Shut Up	37
5. The Cautionary Tale of Lemony Sourpuss	45
6. Hag	53
7. The Last Sister	59
8. The Last Days of Gomorrah	65
9. The Stray Astronaut	75
10. Death and the Sad Girl	93
11. Swarm	101
12. The False Prophet and the False Teeth	123
13. Keeping Geoffrey's Head	129
14. The Tower	141
15. Mythica	169
16. First Day Jitters	179
17. Buddha's Delight	187
Acknowledgements	219
About the Author	221

Copyright© 2020 by Michael "Kwezi" Ferguson. All rights reserved.

No part of this publication may be reproduced, distributed, or transmitted in any form or by any means, including copying and pasting, photocopying, recording or other electronic or mechanical methods, without the prior written permission of the publisher, except in the case of brief quotations and embodied in in critical reviews and certain other non-commercial uses permitted by copyright law. For permission requests, write to the publisher addressed "Attention: Michael "Kwezi" Ferguson at michaeljohnferguson13@gmail.com

Front cover: www.goonwrite.com

Back cover and spine: Ane Bobbert

Story editor: Ryan Ferguson

Copy editor: Catherine Bower

This is a work of fiction. Names, characters, businesses, places, events, locales and incidents are either the product of the author's imagination or used in a fictitious manner. Any resemblance to actual persons, living or dead, or actual events is purely coincidental.

I seriously had to put this bit in 'cause a guy actually threatened to sue me once.

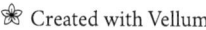 Created with Vellum

*For my grandmothers, **Maureen Ferguson** who taught me to love stories and **Annaline Nel** who made me want to write them. And for **Ouma Fourie**, whose capacity to love is as bottomless as her cookie jar.*

FOREWORD

Ephemera
/ɪˈfɛm(ə)rə,ɪˈfiːm(ə)rə/
noun
Things that exist or are enjoyed for only a short time.

Dear Reader,

If happy endings are what you are looking for then you have come to the wrong place.

I have always been more interested in the darker side of stories. The stories I grew up with always left me wondering. What about the enchantress who put the curse on the prince in the first place? Where did she come from? I wanted to know more about her. When aliens attack a planet, what goes through their minds? Are they merely hateful dominant creatures who want to destroy everything or are they deeper than that? Maybe they are just doing their jobs. There was always a small part of me that wanted the witch to eat Hansel and Gretel. And again, what about the witch? She was evil, no doubt about it, but I wanted to know more about her.

FOREWORD

What happens after the virgins are sacrificed to the volcano if no handsome hero is around to rescue them? In a world obsessed with popular culture, what does a god do when there is no one left who believes in them?

If you are looking for possible answers to these and a few other questions, *then* you have come to the right place.

These are not the kind of stories that get told so they ended up becoming the kind of stories I want to tell. These are the leftovers and afterthoughts that deserve as much attention as the bigger stories they are sometimes only a small part of.

Storytelling is important to me and I wanted to share it in a way that is easily digestible and quick. We live in a world not of magic but of technology where content is consumed faster than it can be created. It's becoming more difficult for storytellers to compete with the ping of a smartphone notification or the ever effective lure of a social media feed. This thought brought me to Ephemera, things that exist, used or enjoyed for only a short time. The stories in this collection are by their very nature ephemeral, however I hope the messages contained within them or the joy they bring are anything but. I invite you to put your electronic devices down and take a break from your world to go on a journey through the worlds that exist in these pages.

Michael Ferguson

Instagram: kweziferguson
Twitter: @KweziFerguson
Goodreads: Michael Ferguson
YouTube: Michael Kwezi Ferguson

1
CHOKE, GASH, UMBRA, CRISPY AND CAROL

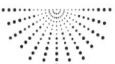

Carol Pumpernickel knew a lot more than people gave her credit for. For example, she knew that she was far from the prettiest girl in school, in fact she was one of the ugliest. This was something she knew because the other children would never let her forget it. It also didn't help that she was among her school's poorest students. Mama did a lot of stuff she wasn't supposed to while she was pregnant. The doctors said that was the reason Carol was held back in school a couple years. People thought that she was stupid, but she was just quiet.

She didn't know so much about English or mathematics or even how to make friends, but there were other things that Carol knew. Things that if people knew Carol knew they would be unhappy, perhaps even angry. Things that her friends in the house would tell her, and therein lies our story.

Carol knew that Monica Russo touched herself while looking at videos of men doing dirty things to one another. She also knew Monica didn't want her boyfriend Brad to know about it. But there was also something Brad didn't want Monica to know: that he was doing dirty things to Monica's mother. Dean Fry from Homeroom enjoyed killing small animals. He took them apart, trying to keep them alive as long as possible and then put them back together again. He enjoyed making them feel pain. It was because his daddy drank and beat his mama. Dean didn't want to feel pain so he made the animals feel it for him. When he thought about killing a person for the first time, it gave him an erection.

They got the house dirt cheap, that's how Carol and Mama could afford to live there. Before the house they lived in a trailer park. When Grandad died eight years ago he left Mama some money and she used it to buy the house. Mama was always taking things no one else wanted and, sometimes, Carol felt like one of those things. It wasn't a nice house like the kind you see on TV. On the outside the paint had long peeled off the walls, some of the windows were broken and weeds grew from the gutters and chimney. The weeds grew tall and straight up, like they were trying to get away from the house. The inside wasn't much better. The parquet flooring had passed its glory days. The wooden panels were rotted and splintery, some had come loose and some were long gone. The walls were faded and stained and some had started to crumble from the damp. It was a sad house, but it was better than living in the trailer park.

Carol didn't think there was anything special about the house until she met her first friend. Carol was in the basement playing dolls when he peeped out from behind a stack of old paint cans. She wasn't afraid of him because of the way he looked, she was afraid he was going to treat her like all the other children had always done.

"Hello," he said from behind the paint cans. He spoke

like the wind blowing through a half open window. He then slowly came out of hiding and Carol got a good look at him. He didn't look like the other boys Carol knew. He was so skinny and so pale that Carol thought if she looked at him hard enough she would see right through him. He looked sick, like he was dying or something and she worried he would give her whatever he had. He had a deep blue bruise all the way around his neck, a mark left by something that had been tied very tightly. His clothes weren't the newest or the cleanest she had ever seen, but she was the last person to make judgements on that kind of thing. Maybe he also had a Mama who didn't have a lot of money and didn't do laundry as often as she should. Maybe he was like her?

"Hi," said Carol cautiously, holding onto her dolls a little tighter. She knew all too well that other children liked to take her toys away from her and sometimes even break them. That's why she liked to play in the basement where no one would bother her, no one would hurt her.

"I like your dolls," he said coming closer. "What are their names?"

Carol's grip on her dolls tightened but she answered, "They aren't so great. Mama got them for me at a jumble sale." She held up the brunette with the wonky eye. "This is Francesca, she likes to drink tea and sing songs." Then she held up the frizzy-haired blonde. "This is Vanessa, she drinks vodka, smokes a lot of cigarettes and sleeps until noon. She's a lot like Mama."

"I think they are cool," he said. "Can I play with you?"

Carol thought she should say that boys aren't supposed to play with dolls but she thought that was a stupid rule.

Anybody should be able to do whatever they like, as long as they didn't hurt anyone else.

"Are you going to hurt me?" she said.

"Why would I do that?" he asked plainly.

"All the other children do," she said, looking down at her shoes.

"All the other children should be kicked in the head until their skulls crack open," the boy replied.

This made Carol laugh. "I'm Carol," she said.

"I'm Choke."

"Would you like to play with Francesca or Vanessa?" Carol asked, holding up both dolls for him to choose from. This was new to her, willingly offering up a toy to share instead of having it ripped away from her.

"Vanessa please," Choke said.

A few weeks passed and soon the highlight of Carol's day was getting home from school and heading down to the basement where she could play with her new friend. Carol and Choke filled the afternoons with tea parties and games of Hide and Seek. Choke was very good at it. No matter how carefully Carol picked her hiding spot it never took Choke long to find her. Finding Choke, on the other hand, took Carol what felt like forever sometimes. After a while it was decided that he wasn't allowed to hide inside the walls anymore because it gave him an unfair advantage.

"Choke," said Carol in the middle of one of their tea parties, "you are my only friend."

"I don't have to be," said Choke as he poured himself his third cup of imaginary tea. "There are lots of us. We are just a bit shy. I can introduce you if you like?"

"Are they all nice like you?"

"Some of them are nicer," he said, taking a sip from his teacup.

Carol thought for a moment. It would be nice to make new friends but she was also scared. If they were all as nice as Choke said they were, then what was there to be afraid of?

"I want to meet them," she eventually said.

Choke put his tea cup down and looked directly at her with his pale blue eyes. "Then you have to do something for me first. But don't worry," he said, "it's easy peasy."

"What do you need me to do?" asked Carol, taking a sip of imaginary tea.

"My friends are stuck somewhere else," said Choke, "and they need someone like you to help them find their way here."

"What do you mean, someone like me?" asked Carol. Was he making fun of her? She couldn't tell. He seemed so serious.

"You are special," said Choke.

Carol liked hearing that she was special. She liked it so much she didn't even care what Choke meant by it. No one had ever said it to her before, if they had then she would have remembered it. "What do I have to do?" she asked eagerly.

Choke produced a stick of purple chalk from his pocket and held it up, "You need to draw a door."

"A door?" asked Carol.

"A special door. The kind of special door that only someone special like you can draw. I will help you."

Carol thought that this was very strange indeed but it didn't stop her from going all in. "Let's do it. Where do you think a good place would be?"

"That wall over there will do just fine," said Choke, pointing to the back wall of the basement.

Choke handed the stick of chalk to Carol. It was the big, fat kind that you use to draw on driveways and pavements. It glittered in her hand and was heavier than the sticks of chalk she'd held before. Her hands started to sweat. She wasn't much of an artist. What if she did it wrong and Choke didn't want to be her friend anymore?

"Don't worry," said Choke. "It will be okay, I'll help you." He stood behind her, gently took her hand and guided it towards the grey wall. Time slowed down for Carol as she watched the chalk scrape along the wall, leaving a glittering trail of purple curls and swirls in its wake. She had no idea how long they had been drawing when Choke loosened his grip on her hand.

"It's done," he said with a wide grin on his powdery face.

Carol took a few steps back from the wall to admire their work. She tilted her head and squinted at the purple chalk drawing. "It doesn't look like a door to me."

They had drawn a large circle with three smaller circles inside. In between each circle, going all the way around was writing. As bad as Carol was at school, even she could see that it wasn't English. It looked more like the picture writing the ancient Egyptians used in their pyramids. In the middle of the drawing was an eye.

"It's perfect," said Choke. He seemed different to Carol. He was looking at the wall the way Mama looked at an unopened bottle of vodka. Carol looked again, trying to see what Choke saw. The markings began to glow. The glow grew brighter until all the markings bled into one and Carol couldn't tell them apart anymore. It was now a purple glowing hole in the wall and creatures started to step through.

The others were arriving. More friends for Carol to play with. They looked very strange but Carol didn't say anything. People had been commenting on her appearance for years and she knew how much it could hurt a person's feelings.

The first to come through the glowing door was a girl. At least Carol thought she was a girl because she had long hair that covered her face and went all the way to her ankles. She was skinny and grey like Choke but her skin was overrun with deep cuts and grazes. She had a funny walk too, like her legs didn't work or it hurt her to move.

"This is Gash," said Choke. "She doesn't speak much but she is very sweet."

Carol wondered if Gash would let her comb and braid her long, black hair.

The second friend to come through the door was a tall shadow with horns and eyes that glowed yellow. He was a towering opaque darkness and the air in the basement grew cold upon his arrival.

"This is Umbra," said Choke. "He is very smart. He knows everyone's secrets. He can tell you all the things people don't want you to know."

The third to emerge from the door was a charred and bloody figure with oozing wounds. His flesh had been incinerated and what was left behind was standing in front of Carol now.

"And this is Crispy," said Choke.

Crispy made a wheezing sound and smoke poured from his mouth. His striking blue eyes stared at Carol.

Carol smiled, "We are *definitely* going to need more tea cups."

Ω

Carol began to spend every moment of spare time she had in the basement with her new friends. She learned that there was no need to be nervous of them because Gash, Umbra and Crispy were just as nice to her as Choke was. They played her games and even taught her some special games of their own.

Gash taught her how to move things without touching them.

Umbra showed her how to see things when she looked at a person, but especially the things that they didn't want anyone to know.

Crispy showed her how to set fire to things just by thinking about it. They practiced on matches and made a game out of it.

Choke showed her how to get people to do things she wanted. They started by practicing on spiders in the basement. Carol took to it naturally and found that within a few days she could make the spiders do backflips and run around. She and Choke would have races to see who could make their spider run the fastest.

Mama didn't notice anything. When she was not passed out drunk she was grateful that Carol wasn't in her way, especially when she had one of her man friends over. Carol hated it when Mama brought men into the house. The man would disappear with Mama into her room and they wouldn't come out for hours. Sometimes Carol could hear moaning coming from the room and other times crying. It wasn't so much the men coming over that Carol had a problem with but rather the way Mama would be after the men left. Sometimes Mama would be sad and just lie in her bed for the rest of the day, crying. Other times, Mama would be in a terrible mood and break things in the house. It scared Carol.

One afternoon while Carol and her friends were in the basement playing a game of Matches, they heard a lot of noise coming from Mama's room. It was so loud Carol couldn't concentrate on lighting her match, something that she normally had no trouble doing. She frowned and threw the unlit match to the ground.

The friends were quiet until Choke decided to say something. "We can make him go away if you like. Somewhere so far he will never come back."

"How?" asked Carol.

"We can do lots of things," said Gash.

"You don't just want him to go away," said Umbra. "You want him to suffer."

Carol nodded.

"We can make that happen too," said Gash, with a smile across her slashed up face.

They waited until they heard Mama's bedroom door open. The man was letting himself out.

"I'll get him" said Gash.

"What if Mama sees you?" Carol asked in a panic.

"She won't." Gash sounded very confident and Carol didn't want to argue with her.

Gash started up the stairs of the basement and the closer she got to the door the more her looks changed. The cuts and slices closed and healed, leaving behind perfect healthy skin, free of scars. Her long hair was the cleanest Carol had ever seen it. Gash looked prettier than even the prettiest girl at school. Once she was at the top of the stairs, Gash turned back to look at Carol. Gash smiled and put her index finger to her plump, red lips, signalling Carol to be still. The door clicked and Gash slipped into the main body of the house.

Gash was not gone long before the door opened again. Carol hid behind the stack of paint cans where she had first met Choke. The rest of her friends vanished into the shadows where they hid best. She had a pretty good view of the basement if she stayed on her haunches and peeped between the gaps in the cans. Gash was on her way down again, still looking beautiful. The man was following her. He was heavy and the wooden stairs creaked loudly under his weight. Carol could smell the booze on him before he even got to the foot of the stairs. She wanted to use the tricks Umbra had taught her, she wanted to look inside of him and see all his dirty secrets but she stopped herself. It was better that she didn't look. She might find something that would deeply disturb her.

"It's no wonder Vanessa keeps you hidden away," the man slurred. He had not even bothered to do his belt up properly. "If I had known she had such a sexy little thing for a daughter I would have started coming to you ages ago. Vanessa is great and all but that crashmat has had a few poundings too many, if you know what I mean." The man chortled at his own joke and Gash looked over her shoulder at him with a look that beckoned him closer.

"You wanna do it in here?" he asked.

Gash nodded in response.

"Whatever you like, sweet pea," he said while unzipping his fly and letting his trousers fall around his ankles.

As Gash turned to face the man she returned to her true form of slash-ridden skin and matted hair, but there was something different this time. Her eyes were aflame with a sick yellow light and her sweet smile had given way to a mouthful of hideous sharp teeth. "Give it to me, daddy," she said in a deep voice that did not belong to her.

The man snorted as he tripped over his own pants, hitting his head against the concrete floor with a whack that echoed through the basement. Gash drew closer to him and he looked on in terror as hundreds of thin, purple tentacles emerged from the cuts on her body. The man tried to scream but could only muster a strained moan. All the colour had gone from his face and his eyes were wide with terror. Gash's slimy tentacles grew longer still and slithered towards him, winding their way around his body and caressing his face. He was still trying to scream but was unable to make anything more than a long, high-pitched squeak. A foul-smelling smoke began to rise from his skin as the tentacles melted his clothes and flesh. They were wrapped around him tightly, now restricting his movement to sharp shudders and squirms of pain. He stopped moving before the rest of his flesh melted away, until there was nothing left of him but a small black puddle on the basement floor.

"Are there others?" asked Umbra.

"What others?" Carol asked.

"Others who have hurt you," said Gash as the tentacles drew back inside her body. Her chest was heaving like she'd just run a marathon.

"Others who have made you suffer," said Choke

"Others who you want to make pay," rasped Crispy in his smoke ravaged voice.

Carol thought of all the children at school and in the neighbourhood who made fun of her because she was slow. The ones who called her ugly and broke her toys. She thought of all the people who made her feel alone. Then she looked at her four new friends who had shown her kindness and had defended her. "Yes," she replied.

"Bring them to us," the new friends said in chorus. "Use what we have taught you and bring them to us. Bring them all to us and we will make them pay."

So she did.

2

MURKY WATERS

$\mathcal{F}$āxiàn stood on his boat and looked over the deep muddy waters of the Yellow River, his small red fishing boat rocked gently near the bank. If only it were fish they had come in search of.

The sun had not begun to rise but the birds in the trees on the riverbanks were wide awake. They chirped and squawked and cheeped, letting each other and the rest of the world know they had made it through another night. The old boatman leaned on his oar, lit a cigarette and took a long drag, making the ember on the end glow brilliant red.

David rubbed his eyes. "No one should be up at this time of the morning."

"I'm afraid he's not much of a talker," said Jiang. They were both standing on the riverbank waiting for Fāxiàn to invite them onto the boat.

"That might be a bit of a problem," said David, "seeing as I've been sent here to interview him. But I guess that's what I have you for." David was surprised his editor signed off on paying for an interpreter and guide whose English was so good. Jiang had been the only good thing to happen to David on this trip so far. His flight had been crowded and everyone he had met since arriving in China had been unfriendly, with the exception of Jiang. The crack house of a hotel David was staying in was a cockroach-infested hellhole with broken air conditioning. When David saw the Western style toilet in his room he counted it as a blessing until he noticed the leak coming from the U-bend.

"He told me that he didn't want to do the interview," said Jiang.

David chuckled. "Well my editor told me he didn't want to do the interview *for free*."

"Money talks around here," said Jiang, shrugging. "Lanzhou is a desperate place riddled with poverty and crime, people do what they must to survive."

"And is that how our friend here," said David motioning toward Fāxiàn, "came into this grizzly profession?"

"He is just one in a whole group of men who go corpse fishing here," said Jiang. "They all have their own reasons but the money is definitely the main one."

"Five hundred dollars a body you say?" David asked, getting his notepad out.

"Sometimes more if the person is from a wealthy family or an important politician," said Jiang.

"Politicians end up in this river?" David asked, taking notes.

"You would be surprised," said Jiang. "The Yellow River does not claim the life of every corpse that finds its way to the water. The river is used as a dumping ground for murder victims, those who take their own lives and those who nobody wants to be responsible for any longer. The people in the region know, if someone you love is missing, the river is the first place you come looking for them."

"Why does it smell so bad?" asked David. The stench draped in the air like the tattered curtains in the windows of all the hovels he had driven past on his way to the river.

"People treat the river like a dump," said Jiang. "The smell is mostly from the abattoirs dumping whatever pig meat they can't use into the river but there is a lot of other pollution as well. The wet market stall owners throw their leftover stock in too. Some people call this river the Mother of the Nation, but most call it the River of Sorrow. It has flooded and changed course more times than people can remember and claimed many lives every time."

"And knowing all of this we are still going to climb on a boat and row right into the middle of all the dead bodies and pig guts and sorrow?" David asked.

"That's what you wanted right?" asked Jiang. "A day out on the river with a corpse fisherman?"

"What I want is a Pulitzer Prize in journalism," said David, "but I guess this beats getting blown to smithereens by an IED in Afghanistan."

David's young tour guide shook his head and let out a laugh that came from the bottom of his stomach. "You Westerners are so funny! Even better than in the movies." Jiang's smile was the widest thing about him, the man looked like someone dressed a stick insect in a button up shirt and baseball cap. There wasn't an inch of the guy that wasn't sinewy and angular. It was a good smile, genuine and full and he had all his teeth, which is more than could be said for Fǎxiàn. Earlier the corpse fisherman had yawned and David counted a total of five brittle warn down teeth.

Fǎxiàn thumped his oar into the floor of the boat and called out to Jiang in Chinese. His voice was gruff from a lifetime of strong tobacco and baijiu.

"He says it's time to go," said Jiang.

David had never been comfortable on water, much preferring dry land. He didn't like all the unsteady rocking under his feet or how he couldn't see what was going on beneath the surface. Taking a deep breath and making sure the life jacket he had brought from home was securely fastened, he stepped off the riverbank and into the rickety boat. The appearance of the boat had not instilled much confidence when David was on land but now that he was actually inside, he had no idea how they were staying afloat. Water spilled in over the sides and soaked David's shoes.

"Don't worry," said Jiang. "This is a calm part of the river where everything that falls in comes to settle. There is no danger here."

David looked out over the light brown waters of the river softly swerving past its banks. He wondered what kind of horrors it secretly carried under the cover of silt. "I'll try keep that in mind," he said.

The sun was making its appearance, casting its light over the river and aiding Fǎxiàn in his search for bodies in the water. A rattle made its way up David's spine and the hair on his arms stood at attention.

Fǎxiàn dipped his oar into the water and set the boat in motion. David was glad he had come in summer. It did mean the smell of rot was worse but at least he wasn't freezing his ass off. He watched Fǎxiàn row while his wrinkle-framed eyes scanned the river, paying close attention to the low hanging branches growing from the bank. Jiang said bodies sometimes got caught and tangled up in these branches, bringing their tragic journey down the river to an end.

They travelled gently further down the river guided by Fǎxiàn's steady oaring. It wasn't long before the temperate morning sun turned uncomfortably hot. Sweat poured down David's face and neck, drenching his shirt. He took a swig from the bottle of water he had brought with. It had been nice and chilled when he had bought it earlier that morning but now it was warm and offered little comfort from the cooking heat.

"So out of all the stories you could have been sent on, how did you get this one?" Jiang asked. His tan skin was shiny with a layer of sweat that glistened in the bright sunlight.

"I'm afraid of water and my editor has a sick sense of humour," said David.

"Water is a funny thing to be afraid of," said Jiang, reaching his hand over the side of the boat and holding it against the flow. "If the river is flooding then it's good to be afraid, but other than that, there is nothing to fear."

"Yeah well there isn't anything funny about drowning," said David.

"Don't you know how to swim?" Jiang asked, drying his hand off on his cargo pants and pointing at David's life jacket.

"I can swim fine," said David, "This is just a precaution." He tugged on the straps of the lifejacket.

"Then why are you so nervous?" Jiang pried.

David bit his bottom lip. He didn't want to make a fool of himself but his face was betraying him. What did it matter anyway? This time tomorrow he'd be on his way back home, never to see Jiang again. "There was an incident," said David. "When I was very young – about five or six. My family went on holiday to the seaside and I nearly drowned. It's not a debilitating fear, I'm just not very comfortable around large bodies of water."

"Oh…" said Jiang. "I was going to give you some facts about the river but now I think it's best if I don't say."

"I'm a big boy," said David, straightening his posture. "I can handle it."

Jiang shrugged, "Legend says the river never really gives up her dead. Even if the bodies are recovered their spirits are forever trapped inside her waters."

David frowned. "Yeah, maybe you are right. Let's keep the facts to a minimum."

Fǎxiàn began to speak to Jiang in Chinese and for the first time it was more than just one or two words. While he spoke he didn't look away from the water.

"He says his son was taken by the river," Jiang translated. "It happened during a flood many years ago. His son's body was never found. That's why he became a corpse fisherman, so that he can be close to his son. He searches the river to provide people with the closure and comfort that he never had."

David made notes of Fǎxiàn's words. It was good material, the kind of thing his editor went gaga for. That and the fact that the man and others like him were getting paid five hundred dollars a body.

Fāxiàn's attention was caught by something and he leaned forward in the boat before pointing to a section of the riverbank.

"He's found a body," said Jiang.

Fāxiàn steered the boat towards the left bank of the river where a corpse floated facedown, caught in the low hanging branches of a nearby tree. The boat drew closer and Fāxiàn got up, picking up a pole with a thick metal hook duct taped to the end. He reached over with the pole and got hold of the corpse. The blunt hook tore right through the flesh, impaling the side of the body just below the armpit.

Fāxiàn pulled the swollen waterlogged corpse closer to the boat and the smell hit David like a punch to the face. The stench of rot was so sickening and overwhelming David's stomach did cartwheels. It wasn't the kind of smell that knocked politely at your nostrils and gently wafted in. It was the kind of smell that broke the door down and forced itself all the way down your throat. It made the air thick and heavy with death. It got behind your eyes and saturated your vision.

Fāxiàn leaned over the side of the boat making the whole thing tilt in the water. David grabbed hold of the side, driving dry splinters into both his palms but this didn't stop him from tightening his grip. When the top half of the fisherman's body reappeared inside the boat it pulled the corpse on board with it. David backed away as far as he could without letting go of the side of the boat. The vessel was now rocking back and forth harder than ever. David was convinced it would capsize.

The boat settled with the dead body lying face up inside, not that it had much of a face left. Crabs and fish had eaten away at the eyes and lips, creating a disturbing smile on what

David thought must have once been a woman's pretty face. Her long black hair lay in wet clumps and tangles over her chest.

Fāxiàn went straight back to rowing, business as usual. With the boat finally stable David let go, his splintered hands oozing blood.

"I have a first aid kit in my scooter," said Jiang. "I can help you get that cleaned up."

"Thanks," said David, unable to take his eyes off the dead woman. Her head was twisted away from him at an unnatural angle. Her skin was a waxy grey colour under the torn up summer dress that clung to her. Covering his mouth and nose with his bloodied hand, he leaned in a little closer to get a better look. He had never been this close to a dead person before.

"It's so strange," he said to Jiang. "To think that this was a person with a life, friends and family and now she's just this hollow thing lying in front of us. What do you think happened to her?"

Jiang shrugged. "I'm not a doctor but her neck looks broken. She could have been murdered, but depending on how far up river she was from, if she jumped from a bridge it could have broken when she hit the water."

David leaned in even closer. A fly was crawling on the swollen remnants of her cheek. It rubbed its legs together before disappearing inside her empty eye socket. David drew closer, his eyes trying to follow the fly in.

The corpse then turned its neck with a loud pop, looked straight at him and said through its lipless mouth, "Will you be mine?"

David flew backwards, rocking the boat and losing his

balance. The sound he made was a harsh wheeze caused by air entering his throat in a hard gasp instead of leaving it in a scream. David's back hit the water and he went under. Instead of floating back up like he expected, something wrapped itself around his ankle and pulled him further down. The lifejacket pushed up against David's neck, its sharp seams grating against his skin. He opened his eyes and looked down to try see what was pulling him. The few beams of sunlight that broke through the silt and danced in the water were of little help. All David could see below him was an abyss from which nothing ever returned. The darkness was reaching out to him like withered hands trying to grab at his life and take it for themselves. He kicked against the force that clung to his ankle, reached down at it, tried to knock it away but it was no good. He sank further and his lungs began to burn for breath.

He was dragged towards small balls of yellow light that were emerging from the abyss, floating like seeds on a breeze. They were not the same yellow as sunshine or candle light. These glowing orbs shone the colour of jaundice, pus and bile. His chest was ready to burst. He did not know how much longer he could resist taking in two lungful's of water and sealing his fate. Something grabbed David around the waist and pulled him upward, breaking the grip on what was holding his ankle. His body broke the surface of the water with a splash and he took a massive gulp of air. He was back in the boat with Jiang and Fāxiàn standing over him. He looked to his right. The body of the woman was lying next to him.

"Thank you," he spluttered. "I was in so deep, I couldn't get out, and something was pulling me down."

"What are you talking about?" Jiang asked. "You fell in and were floating face down in the water the whole time. Your body never even went completely under the surface."

"What?" David asked sitting up. He scooted away from the dead body and sat against the side of the boat, water dripping from his hair.

"We thought you had passed out or something," said Jiang. "Why did you fall out the boat?"

David looked at the body of the woman. "I don't know," he said wiping the water off his face, not wanting to sound any crazier than he already did.

Ω

THE RIDE to the cove was silent. David sat facing away from the body and kept his eyes on the floor of the boat. He didn't want to look at the river either. He just wanted the trip to be over. Jiang explained that Fāxiàn took the bodies to the cove so they would be protected from the current. The small cove was also used as a meeting point for loved ones to identify and pay for the salvaged bodies.

The cove was little more than a small sheltered riverbank that cradled the water. Thanks to the way the river had formed the current there was almost non-existent. The trees and foliage grew thick and wild on this part of the riverbank. David realised for the first time how isolated they were out here. He wondered who would come looking for their bodies if something happened to them. The sun was high but grey clouds had begun to roll in, bringing some relief from the heat. David wished for rain.

"So what happens now?" David asked as the boat rocked gently in the shallow water.

"We wait," said Jiang. "Fāxiàn has arranged with a family looking for a lost loved one to meet here soon."

"Why don't the police handle this?" David asked. "The whole thing feels illegal and to be honest, extortionist."

"So much for objective journalism," said Jiang. "I hope you don't let your bias opinions pollute your article. People are happy to pay Fāxiàn. They are happy to have found their loved ones, happy to have closure and Fāxiàn is happy to be able to pay his bills. The cops here don't care anyway, they use missing person's reports for toilet paper. Even if the police did handle it, then Fāxiàn and the rest of the boatmen would lose out on money. The cops have their hands full with serious crime."

"I'm sorry," said David, truly embarrassed, especially at his journalistic integrity being called into question. "You are right. I shouldn't judge, I'm not from around here so I wouldn't understand."

They waited in more silence as the clouds rolled in thicker and darker while thunder rumbled in the distance. Fat drops of rain began to beat down from the sky, hitting the river in a million little explosions. The three men and the corpse in the boat were drenched in seconds. They remained in the boat just off the shore until a flashing light blinked at them from the bushes. This was apparently the signal Fāxiàn had been waiting for. As soon as he saw the light he paddled the boat onto the shore. David climbed out of the boat and his feet sank into the sticky claylike mud of the wet river bank.

"It would be best if we wait here while he conducts his business," said Jiang.

"Fair enough," said David.

Fāxiàn grabbed the body of the dead woman under her arms and dragged her from the boat, her bare heels digging tracks in the mud. Fāxiàn set the body down while Jiang and David waited a few meters away. The rain was coming down harder and David shivered. Two people emerged from the bushes, a man and a woman wearing thick rain jackets. Fāxiàn showed them to the body and they stood silent for a moment before the woman began to wail into the man's arms. The man kept his composure and negotiated with Fāxiàn over the sobs of the woman. Her face remained buried in the man's shoulder, her body shuddering with grief. Fāxiàn took an envelope from the man and opened it to count the bouquet of bank notes it contained. Fāxiàn nodded at the man before they shook hands and the man waved at the bushes. Two men appeared carrying a stretcher and a sleeping bag. They wrapped the body up and loaded it onto the stretcher before carrying it off into the bushes and out of site. The man and woman bowed to Fāxiàn and he bowed back before they too disappeared into the bushes.

"Looked like closure to me," said David, "or something like it."

Jiang nodded at David but didn't say anything.

David clapped his hands together. "I guess we can call it a day then. Let's go, I need to get out of this rain." Both he and Jiang turned to head back to the boat.

"You can't go yet," said Fāxiàn in perfect English. "She is not finished with you."

David and Jiang turned back at the same time.

"You speak English," said David stunned.

"There is a lot about me you don't know, Westerner," said Fāxiàn.

David and Jiang had been so surprised they didn't notice the sticky mud beneath their feet slowly grow softer and stickier. The mud bubbled over their shoes and slithered up their legs, pinning them in place. David tugged and yanked and pulled but he was stuck.

"What the hell is going on?" David yelled trying to free his legs. Jiang had started wailing in Chinese at a panicked speed. David didn't need to speak the language to understand what was going on. A man begging for his life sounds the same in any tongue. The inside of David's mouth went dry and adrenaline coursed through his body, tightening his muscles and making his heart clobber.

Jiang raised his trembling arm and pointed his finger at Fāxiàn. "Shuǐ guǐ!" he moaned. It was the only word David could pick up because he kept screaming it over and over again. "Shuǐ guǐ! Shuǐ guǐ!" The colour had been snatched from Jiang's skin, leaving him as pale as the full moon. His face overflowed in a quivering mess of tears and mucus.

"You both belong to the river now," said Fāxiàn. "And once she has your souls, your bodies will belong to me."

"You can't do this!" said David. "People will come looking for us!"

"They most definitely will," said Fāxiàn. "And when they do, I will charge them a handsome sum for each of you. But first, she will have you." The old boatman pointed a filthy finger to the silt saturated waters of the river, still being pelted by rainfall.

"After my son disappeared in the flood," Fāxiàn continued. "I came out here looking for him. I spent days combing the waters and searching the banks for his body. On the third day I searched until after it got dark. That was when she called out to me the first time. She told me things, things no man is meant to know. I could not escape her, I was not even safe in my dreams. She would call to me. She promised if I brought enough souls to her waters that she would one day reunite me with my son. She would show him to me in her waves and ripples. I would catch just a glimpse of his face, but I know she still has him, somewhere deep down there in the cold and the dark. You will help me see my son again and you will help make me money too."

The sticky polluted mud climbed further up David and Jiang's bodies, making its way over their torsos. A force yanked David by his ankles and he knew it immediately. It was the same cold grip that he had experienced earlier that day when he had fallen into the river. He lost his balance and fell to the mud. He went down first, followed shortly by Jiang. They were being pulled by the mud into the river. David grabbed at the river bank trying to fight the invisible tow rope tied to his ankles but came away with mud, clay and small rocks that broke off in his hands. He looked back at the small waves lapping at his feet, beckoning him and his guide closer and closer. He watched the mud crawl up Jiang's neck as he shrieked and tried to claw away from the river. The mud saw his open mouth as an invitation to creep inside and start choking him. Panic coiled around David's chest, getting tighter, his heart was thumping so loud and so fast he thought it might explode. He wanted to scream too but didn't want to suffer the same fate as Jiang.

He twisted his head to look up at Fāxiàn. "Please," he

begged, "don't do this! I don't want to die! I don't want to die like this!"

"The river calls to me," said the old boatman. "She demands sacrifice. She hungers for more souls."

David's body slid into the river and he was pulled under. He disappearing without a trace save for the last few air bubbles that broke the surface of the murky water.

3
THORNS

You may remember the story of an evil witch and the Prince she cursed to be a monster forever. Where I come from, it is told a little differently.

Fairy politics and etiquette are understood by few mortals, but missteps can cause ramifications that echo through generations. They come to rest in the memories of storytellers the world over and are passed down in front of campfires or before bedtime.

I was told this tale often as I was tucked into bed. Our home was safe and warm. The glow-worm lamplights burned low in the room and I smelled strongly of the rosemary oil and honey-infused soap I used to bathe with.

Long ago, the powerful Kingdom of Ambrosia owed its great wealth to the famous honey it produced. Kingdoms far and wide would purchase the honey en masse, singing its praises. It was even rumoured to have magical properties and was used as an ingredient in many a potion and ointment. People believed that Ambrosian honey could do anything, from healing wounds to bringing back a lost lover whose heart (and perhaps other, more erogenous, organs) had wandered astray. Bakers swore the honey made their cakes taste the sweetest and wise women claimed it made their spells most potent.

Ambrosia bordered another kingdom that was filled with magic and wonder. This was the Kingdom of The Fae, fantastic creatures misunderstood by humans. Mischievous sprites that could dance on rays of sunlight, animals with the gift of speech and even ancient trees that could move around as freely as you or I called the mysterious kingdom home.

Under the human King's rule, the two kingdoms lived in peace and prosperity. In exchange for The Fae not interfering in the affairs of his kingdom, the King would leave a substantial offering of honey at the border every month. The King was wise and knew that as wondrous as fairy magic was, it was also capable of things dark and powerful.

The Prince of Ambrosia was unfortunately not as wise. He couldn't understand his father's attitude towards what the prince considered a weaker kingdom that could easily be overthrown and absorbed into their own for profit and power.

When the Prince asked his father why he allowed the kingdom to give away such large amounts of a valuable resource, the King answered, "That is the way it has always been. My father did it before me and his father before him all the way back as long as anyone can remember."

"My father's head is filled with bees wax," the Prince would say. "He runs this kingdom under the fear of old wives' tales and tall stories."

The King was old and when he became too ill to rule but not yet ill enough to die, Prince Cyprian took over control of the kingdom as King Regent. His first command was to stop the offerings of honey to The Fae. It was instead exported to the kingdoms that paid for it, to generate greater income.

This transgression did not go unnoticed by The Fae. They sent an emissary over the border to the gates of Prince Cyprian's castle. She had the appearance of an old woman, hunched over and wrinkled. The guards did not question her when she requested an audience with the King Regent for there was no denying she was Fae and they were afraid of her. She was dressed in foreign cloth spun from a glittering gossamer unlike any the guards had seen before. If this was not enough to convince them, her features, while human enough not to draw attention, were subtly different. Her eyes were large with dilated pitch-black pupils and irises of glowing amber. The guards knew those eyes could see far more than what was merely in front of them. Her grey hair wisped gently around the edges of her face like pipe smoke suspended in the air on a windless day.

The Fae woman was escorted into the throne room and brought before the Prince, who sat perched on the throne that was not yet truly his.

"It's too big for you," said the old woman, "you still have some growing to do."

"Excuse me?" spat the Prince.

"The throne," said the old woman. "You don't fill it quite right yet. Like a toddler trying to walk around in his father's shoes."

"How dare you speak to me like that!" shouted Prince Cyprian, "Do you know who I am?"

"I know very well who you are, Prince Cyprian of the house of Melisseus, King Regent of the Kingdom of

Ambrosia," said the woman. "But I don't think *you* know who you are."

"What nonsense is this?" asked the Prince. "I shall have your head."

"You shall have nothing of mine," replied the woman calmly. "I have come with a warning. If you do not reinstate the offerings of honey to The Fae, there will be dire consequences for you and the rest of Ambrosia."

"You *dare* threaten me?" said the Prince through clenched teeth. "Guards," he ordered, "seize this crone! I would like to see her executed and her freakishly wrinkled head mounted as a hunting trophy."

"You have been warned," said the woman, before quickly fading out of sight.

Prince Cyprian thought little of the visit from the mysterious Fae woman and went about running the kingdom as he felt it should be. This included no longer leaving the offerings of honey at the border. When the second month came and went without any offering of honey, the old woman appeared before him again.

This time, she did not bother with the castle gate or the guards. Prince Cyprian was in his throne room and when he turned around, there she was. He got quite a fright.

"How did you get in here?" he demanded to know, in a voice that was shaken but still authoritative.

"The same way I got out the previous time," said the old woman. "Your tall stone walls and guarded gates mean nothing to me. I am of The Fae and there is little in your world that can bind me."

"You can't just come in here unannounced!" shouted the Prince.

"I shall do as I please," said the woman. Her amber eyes glowed dangerously and the Prince took a step back. "This is the second month that you have withheld the offerings of honey. I have come to warn you a final time. Reinstate the offerings or bear the consequences."

The Prince puffed out his chest and took a step towards the woman. "You do not warn me, hag! I am the King Regent and I will not be treated this way! Here is a warning for you: if you step a foot inside this castle again, not only will I have your head but I will launch a full scale attack on your kingdom with all the might my army can muster. I will not rest until every Fae in the land is obliterated from existence. Do you understand me?"

The woman did not bat an eye. "You have made yourself crystal clear," she said coldly, before once again disappearing from sight.

As old people often do, the King took a long time to die. He eventually expired, shortly before the end of the third month of the Prince's reign as King Regent. In his haste to have the crown resting comfortably on his head, the Prince decided to forgo the customary mourning period. Arrangements for his coronation were made before his father was even cold in the ground.

It was a glittering affair with no expense spared. Nobility from far and wide had been invited to attend as well as many of Ambrosia's elite. The vows were taken and the rites observed, but at the moment the crown was lowered onto the Prince's head, a great rumble of thunder tore through the throne room. The crown dropped and fell to the stone floor with a clang, rolling into the shadows. An orb of violet light appeared in the room before the Prince. The orb expanded with a bright boom to reveal the old Fae woman standing in its place.

"Prince Cyprian of Ambrosia," said the woman, her voice echoing through the chamber. "You have been found guilty of violating the ancient treaty. I have come to carry out your sentence." Her large amber eyes glowed so brightly that the Prince and party guests had to cover their eyes. The woman's appearance melted away to reveal a beautiful enchantress. She stood before them in ethereal perfection. Tall and graceful, her skin glowed as if lit from within. Her long hair spilled over her shoulders and down her back like molten gold. She raised her arm and pointed her index finger at the Prince. Some of the guests had begun to flee.

"What you do not know," bellowed the enchantress, "is that Ambrosia's honey is such high quality because it's made from the nectar of enchanted flowers from *my* kingdom. But since you feel so strongly about war, you leave The Fae no choice but to defend ourselves."

Prince Cyprian fell from the throne to his knees. Terror flushed his face and his hands flew up in plea.

Violet flames sprung up around the enchantress as she continued. "Hear this! From this day forth, no honeybee shall cross the border from the Kingdom of The Fae into Ambrosia! I curse the land upon which Ambrosia stands. No longer shall her crops flourish, no longer shall her streams bubble. Her trees shall not bear fruit and her air shall no longer carry the sweet scent of flowers."

Her curse arrived in the form of a sudden and terrible thunderstorm that rattled the castle in its foundations. Windows burst open and a cold wind blew out all the candles. The remaining royal court and party guests fled in terror, leaving only the Prince quivering before the enchantress in the dark and empty throne room.

"And for you, arrogant Prince," said the enchantress, as a grin crept across her face, "a special curse." Outside, a dense forest of thorns erupted from the ground and encased the castle so that none could enter or leave. The begging Prince wept as he fell on all fours and transformed into a grotesque creature. His skin changed to the colour of a rotting corpse. His body contorted on the cold stone floor, he looked upon his hands in horror as they twisted into hideous talons before his eyes. His limbs elongated into sinewy rods and all the hair fell from his head. As the transformation neared its end, he caught a glimpse of himself in a nearby mirror. He screamed and an unearthly shriek escaped his throat.

"For you with the heart of a flowerless weed, who would only nourish himself to the detriment of everything around him, here is the kingdom you will inherit from your father and the form in which you will rule forever!"

She conjured a vine of thorns and fashioned it into a band. She then placed the band onto the creature's head and pushed down hard. The Prince whimpered as the sharp spikes pierced his flesh, drawing blood.

"Congratulations on your coronation, your majesty," she said mockingly as she bowed. "It is a fitting crown for the King of Thorns!" The enchantress smirked before she vanished, leaving the Prince alone in his castle, condemned to stalk the shadows for the rest of his unnaturally long existence.

On the night of a full moon, the monster was able to leave the fortress of thorns and prey upon a nearby village, where it would feed on the only thing that could satiate its never-ending hunger – human flesh.

I hear that humans have many stories of their own. Stories of lost civilizations that disappeared without a trace where the only things found were the ruins uncovered centuries later. I wonder if the Kingdom of Ambrosia is one such place to them. They also have stories of monsters that lurk in the shadows waiting to devour them.

The Fae believe that stories are a giant tapestry, the fabrics of which connect us all as they are sewn from one generation into the next. I wonder if the humans are the same, if their tapestry somehow begins where our tapestry ends.

I was told the story of Prince Cyprian on many occasions as a child. And many nights I would fall asleep and dream of human Kings cursed to haunt their own castles forever.

4

IT CAME FROM OUTER SPACE AND WOULDN'T SHUT UP

"Just so you know, I'm not a big fan of the term 'Space Invader'. It makes it sound like I have no respect for personal boundaries and I'm really not that kind of guy."

It was stuffy in the interrogation room and Agent Brommer was coming to the end of his patience. He and Agent Slate had been interrogating the alien for hours and were getting nowhere.

"Enough!" Brommer shouted, slamming his hands down on the metal table, making it rattle. His palms burned. "Tell us why you're here and what you want!"

The alien was not intimidated and gave the judgmental look mothers get when their children throw tantrums in public. Hours of questioning and they had only managed to get his name out of him, information that was useless. Brommer looked upon the alien with disgust. Its slimy, green skin and bulbous, vein-covered head gave him the heebie-jeebies. They were small creatures, skinny, about half the height of an average human, with massive yellow eyes the shape of American footballs. The alien wrapped its four thin green fingers around the drink it had insisted on receiving upon its arrival – an extra-large Coke from McDonalds. It sipped at the drink with its jagged little mouth, making no eye contact as Brommer and Slate looked on.

It finished its sip, then said, "Did your mother never teach you it's considered rude to stare? That's true even on my home world."

"Why are you attacking our planet?" asked Agent Slate. The marathon interrogation was taking a toll on her too. Earth had come under attack by an alien invasion just less than 24 hours ago. Thousands of gigantic ships the shape of nautilus shells appeared in the sky above every continent and chaos shortly ensued. Soldiers on the ground recovered this chatty specimen. The alien vehicle it was riding in had malfunctioned and it was forced to perform an emergency ejection. He was immediately taken prisoner and brought to The Institution for questioning. Brommer and Slate knew the assignment to get information out of him was going to be difficult, but nothing could have prepared them for how annoying the alien had turned out to be.

"It's very presumptuous of you to assume that this is an attack," said Kudzu. "You know nothing about us or our culture, what if this is just how we say hello?"

"Like hell it is!" shouted Brommer.

Kudzu calmly put his drink back on the table. "Let me ask you something. If your boss told you to do something, would you do it? I got a family to support, man. You think humans are the only ones with kids to feed?" The alien clicked his purple tongue, crossed his arms and frowned. "I gotta say, I have taken over *a lot* of worlds in my time but you guys are definitely the most self-absorbed species I have come across."

"I can't believe this," Slate sighed as she walked away, rubbing her temples. She then turned to Brommer. "The fate of humanity depends on the information we can extract from this thing. I would understand if it just sat there not saying anything, but this?"

"Cool it, Agent Slate," said Brommer. The last thing he needed in the middle of an interrogation was a meltdown from his partner.

Kudzu continued to speak. "One time, we took over a planet inhabited by a race of frog people, they didn't even put up a fight, and you know why? They understood that we were just doing our jobs. You guys like to say that we report to the mothership, well guess who runs the mothership? That's right, my boss."

"Let's just torture the information out of him," said Slate, taking off her jacket and rolling up her sleeves. "I'll get my pipe wrench."

"Agents," said Kudzu, "if you so much as lay a finger on me I'll squirt corrosive acid on both of you through my pores."

"You can't do that," said Slate.

"You don't know what I can do," said the alien. "But if you're willing to take the chance, then by all means, go get your pipe wrench and let's find out."

An uncomfortable silence followed before Kudzu smirked, "I didn't think so."

"Just tell us why you're attacking our planet!" shouted Slate.

"Do you think I wanted to be an intergalactic conqueror

of worlds?" asked Kudzu. "Who the hell *wants* that? I wanted to be a dancer, but the health insurance sucks and my parents made me do the responsible thing and get a real job. Do I like it? No. Does it pay the bills? Duh. I actually can't wait to get back to my planet when all of this is over. The family and I just moved to a new house in one of those gated communities, you know the kind that keep the riff-raff out? It's really something. We are having a house warming this weekend. All my buddies are coming over, it's gonna be out of this world."

"I can't with this," said Slate on the verge of tears. "I really would prefer if he just refused to speak instead."

"You know they're coming to get me right? It's not like you can just get away with abducting one of us like this. And they don't knock. They're gonna rip the roof off this place with one of those big robots we ride around in. You saw them, right? The ones with the claws that shoot lasers."

"Let them come," said Brommer. "We aren't going to get what we want out of you anyway. And even if we did, it is probably too late."

"Now that's just the kind of defeatist attitude my species looks for in a less developed race to overpower and steal from," said Kudzu. "But don't worry, Agent Brommer. It'll all be fine in the end. I don't understand why some species act like getting taken over by us is the end of the world. Did you ever consider that we could make things better for you? I've seen some of the movies your kind make about us and to be frank, I'm very offended. That is some hate speech right there. The intolerance!"

"What did you mean 'steal from'?" asked Brommer.

Kudzu looked at the watch-like device attached to his wrist. Its digital display flashed an array of unidentifiable symbols and Brommer found himself instinctively reaching for his Glock.

"Calm down Agent Brommer," said Kudzu, not looking up from the device. "If I wanted you dead, you'd be dead. But I guess there's no harm in me answering your question. " He turned the device off and looked up at them with his yellow football eyes. "We have come to take your sugar."

Slate's face scrunched up in confused disgust. "You are desolating an entire planet for sugar?"

"In any and all forms it comes in," said Kudzu, picking up his Coke and giving it a shake while smiling at them. "Fructose, galactose, maltose – all of it. If it ends in 'tose, it belongs to us now. We've carried out invasions for far less in the past. This one time, we took over a planet because our queen had a fight with their queen over a casserole dish that was never returned. At least that was the official story, but I smell a conspiracy."

"You can't just slaughter us and rob us of all our sugar!" yelled Brommer. He looked up at the video camera in the corner of the interrogation room. "Are you guys getting this?"

"First of all," said Kudzu, "we can do what we like because we're the ones with the giant killer robots. Secondly, we are not going to slaughter all of you, that would be barbaric and unnecessary, but most of all a waste of our resources. And third, have you had a look at the obesity rate of your planet lately? If anything, we are doing your calorie-clogged backsides a big favour. Trust me, our scientists did the research and the data clearly shows Earthlings are in serious need of a strict diet. And if you get some exercise while we chase you around in our robots, then even better."

The alien gave pause as his eyes scanned over the grim expressions plastered on the agents' faces.

"Oh, cheer up you guys!" he shouted excitedly, pushing himself away from the table and throwing his hands in the air. "You aren't considering the advantages of a mass culling like this! I promise you, once this is over, the lucky few hundred million of you left are gonna be so much happier. Sure in the beginning it will be a difficult adjustment. You'll have to clean up all the rubble and corpses but after that you'll be on the up-and-up! Your economies will bloom and your environment will flourish. Fewer people, more space, more food to go around, more jobs and less pollution always make for an overall happier planetary population. We've seen this many times. Obviously there's a strong chance you opt for the dystopian recourse which inevitably leads to the total collapse of society, cannibalism and, eventually, mass extinction, but it's really up to you guys how you choose to handle your apocalypse. My people aren't in the business of telling other beings what to do. Best of all is that all the people you don't like will probably be dead. Sure, some of the ones you do like will also be dead, but life's a trade off! What you gonna do?"

"Did you say there will only be a few hundred million of us left when you are done?" asked Slate.

"Yeah, we normally wipe out around 95% of a population," the alien responded. "Give or take a few million. I don't know, I'm not the numbers guy. He's on the mothership with my boss. Goddamn bean-counter never has to do a stitch of field work and he earns more than me! How's that for a kick in the acid glands?"

Slate and Brommer looked at each other, the colour

drained from their faces and their knees weakened. They both turned to look at Kudzu but said nothing.

"Don't look at me like that," said Kudzu. "The casualties would have been fewer if you people didn't kick up such a fucking fuss. You could've learned a thing or two about submission from the frog people of Amphibia-9."

Vibrations made their way across the soles of Brommer's feet. Subtle at first but then stronger, until the whole room began to shake violently. Dust fell from the ceiling and lamps swung to and fro. A cacophony of metal scraping against metal and crumbling concrete ruptured the air as the floor cracked underneath them.

"Watch out!" shouted Brommer, as he tackled Slate to safety before half the room was ripped away, nearly taking her with it. Choked and blinded by the dust cloud that filled the air, the agents lay on the floor coughing and spluttering. The dust cleared away by a gust of wind revealing one of the giant robots. Another alien, identical to Kudzu, sat inside glaring at them through the concave windshield.

"That would be my ride," said Kudzu, casually, as if the taxi he had called had arrived.

Brommer helped Slate to her feet and they dusted themselves off. A chrome tentacle emerged from the robot and slithered its way towards Kudzu.

"I've enjoyed our time together and I consider you friends, so," said Kudzu, "I'd like to give you two some advice before I go. Find a nice, quiet and safe space to ride this out. It's gonna take a maximum of five Earth days for us to finish our work here and then we'll leave. I know you humans like to think you can control everything with your guns and your missiles but listen to what I'm telling you." He pointed up towards the sky and motioned around with his finger. "All of this, is *way* bigger than you and your little sapiens brains need to accept that."

The tentacle wrapped itself around the alien's waist as Slate and Brommer watched in quiet shock. "Not so tight Talaxia! I'm not a piece of Gorgozian steak!" Kudzu shouted to his counterpart. He then turned to Slate and Brommer for the last time. "Trust me," he said, as he was being lifted out of the ruined room, "this could be so much worse for you guys. Most other aggressive intergalactic species either enslave or experiment on their takeovers. Let me just say that out of all the stuff in your movies I was talking about earlier, the rectal probing is about the only thing you got right. The Kremulans do that. They're fun to party with but are total freaks. If a species has a hole, they want to stick something in it."

The giant robot strutted off into the sunset. Brommer and Slate could do nothing but watch while their world crumbled down around them.

5
THE CAUTIONARY TALE OF LEMONY SOURPUSS

When women are pregnant, they sometimes get strange cravings. Some women will tell you that they crave chocolate pudding at 3 in the morning. Others will tell you in the sweetest, most innocent of voices about how blessed they are because their whole pregnancy they craved nothing but fruit and vegetables. Watch out for those women because they are liars. My own mother took a liking to fish paste and maple syrup sandwiches while I was in her womb.

Melony Sourpuss was not most women. From the moment sperm greeted egg all that woman wanted to do was eat lemons. She would eat them in any form she could get hold of.

She would take her lemons as smoothies, lemon tea and even lemon juice squirted into water. She ate lemon sponge cake, lemon meringue, lemon tart and lemon ice cream. She would consume, by the bucket-load, lemon sherbet and lemon flavoured boiled sweets. She would also drizzle fresh lemon juice over her salads and fish.

Once, during the pregnancy, while fetching her car from the car wash down the street, she was even tempted to take a bite out of the lemon-scented air freshener the cleaners had hung on her rear-view mirror. She would have done it too were it not for her husband, Norman Sourpuss. He watched the wheels turning in his wife's head. She was poised, like an Olympic diver about to leap. The air freshener (which also happened to be shaped like a lemon and was lemon-yellow in colour) was half way to her wide open mouth. He smacked it from her hand and it flew out the open car window. It hit the tar without making a sound.

"What on Earth did you do that for?" shrieked Melony.

"Are you serious?!" Norman retorted. "You were about to eat the damn thing!"

Things got worse from there. Towards the end of the pregnancy, Norman caught Melony sitting in a corner of the dimly lit pantry eating lemon after lemon as if they were apples. She would consume them, skin and all, in a deranged euphoria without so much as pulling a face.

Melony started to give off the smell of freshly cut lemons. You could always tell when she was around because you would smell her before you saw her. This was neither a good nor bad thing, but rather an interesting side-effect of her self-inflicted condition.

The trouble was that all the lemons in Melony's system raised the acidity levels in her blood and this made for quite the abnormality when it came time to give birth to her child.

When Melony's water broke, she was standing in the garden watering a flower bed. The fluid that came out of that woman was so acidic the grass it fell upon instantly curled up and died. To this day nothing has ever grown there again. It is just a patch of red dirt in the shape of a psychiatrist's ink blot.

The labour was strained and long but the delivery room smelled divine.

"Did someone light one of those over-priced scented candles?" asked one of the nurses.

"We work with oxygen tanks here, you idiot," said one of the other nurses. She was older and had a lifetime of dealing with stupidity behind her. "No one in their right mind would light an open flame in a hospital. Where did you get your nursing qualification?" she demanded to know.

"Benoni," said the stupid nurse, while making eye contact with the floor.

"That explains a lot," said the grumpy older nurse.

"Can we focus please?" asked the doctor, looking up from in between Melony's spread legs.

"Fine," said the grumpy nurse. "But I am telling you now, if this one screws up I am not filling in a stitch of paperwork. I'm three months away from retirement and I have enough on my plate."

Melony let out a low moan that sounded like a clogged fog horn.

Norman was at Melony's bedside, his fingers being crushed by her hand which the hours of labour had turned into a powerful vice grip.

Four screams, eight pushes and one "I'm going to fucking kill you for doing this to me" later, a baby was born.

She was unlike any creature the world had ever seen. Her skin was the most brilliant shade of yellow, as was her thick and unruly hair. Her ellipsoidal head had done a number on her mother's birth canal and her massive almond shaped eyes were sparkling gold. The texture of her flesh was not that of a normal baby's. Her yellow skin was leathery and dimpled. She did not cry but her face was screwed up tighter than a chastity belt on a nun from the Middle Ages.

"She looks..." said the stupid nurse.

"Just like a lemon," said the grumpy one before passing out cold. Her body hit the hospital floor with a dull thud. Soon after these events, she filled out some paper work and took early retirement.

The baby was named Lemony, a double play on words that her mother was quite proud of. Melony and Norman were stunned but loved her nonetheless. They decided they would raise her as they would have done if she had been born looking like an ordinary child. Aside from her incredibly unusual appearance, Lemony was just that: a normal child. She did not want to eat her vegetables, she would throw temper tantrums if she did not get her way and she did not want to go to sleep when bedtime arrived. She also had a kind and thoughtful side to her, as children do, and was particularly fond of physical displays of affection from her mother and father.

The Sourpuss family were not wealthy. Residing in the middle-class suburb of Clovergreen in the old mining town of Braken, they always had enough to get by but it was an uncomfortable squeeze, especially towards the end of the month. For this reason, when the first journalist arrived and offered Melony a substantial amount of money in exchange for a simple interview and a few pictures of Lemony, she said yes. Little did Melony know that she had opened the floodgates to a media circus that, years later, would culminate in Lemony getting her very own reality television show.

"I was worried in the beginning," Melony could be seen saying on a grainy television screen in a documentary filmed shortly after the first journalist showed up with the first cheque. "Norman and I were both worried that people would make fun of Lemony for her appearance. But we were wrong. The world loves her."

The world did love Lemony, for a time. There were a number of successful years filled with talk show appearances, merchandising, a biographical novel titled *When Life is a Lemon* and even a successful Christmas album called *What's Under the Lemon Tree This Christmas*. The album boasted catchy singles such as *Lemon Tree, Oh Lemon Tree*, *Citrus Night, Have Yourself a Zesty Little Christmas* and *All I Want for Christmas is pH of Around 2.0*.

Unfortunately, as tends to happen, the world grew bored of the little girl who looked like a lemon. Poor Lemony, who was by then in her late teens, faded into obscurity. As the reality show wrapped its final season and the book sales began to dry up, Lemony made the acquaintance of what she thought to be a phenomenally charismatic man.

Pastor Prophet Ezekiel Israel Wadi Musa Nebo Golgotha of The Ministry Church of the Holy Order of the Eternally Burning Bush of Zion. A quick Google search would prove that The Pastor's real name was actually Kurt Koekemoer. He was born in the late 70s in a small town outside East-Jesus-Nowhere in the Free State. Kurt lived a normal life until the age of 17 when, one unfortunate afternoon at a church bake sale, a freak accident occurred. While carrying an assortment of cakes for his aunt, Hester-Susanna Koekemoer, Kurt tripped over a Jack Russel that had got underfoot. The cakes went flying and Kurt fell face first into an exposed tent peg.

The doctors said it was a medical miracle that Kurt survived the accident. Kurt, on the other hand, believed that it was a miracle of faith. He said that while he was unconscious he had received a message from God himself. God told Kurt to change his name, start a ministry and spread his seed by taking as many wives as he could. So Kurt did just that.

Fast forward a number of years (and wives) later, The Pastor was the head of a megachurch where he was raking in the prayers and the money. This is not an exaggeration. Footage from an early 2000s documentary on The Ministry Church of the Holy Order of the Eternally Burning Bush of Zion shows church workers literally raking money off the floor at the foot of the podium with actual garden rakes.

Lemony met The Pastor at a book signing for her biography. He was one of a total of four people who showed up. Lemony, like many woman before her, was mesmerized by The Pastor. She fell in love with him and became one of twenty-four sister wives. Life was good for a few years, until law enforcement agents raided the compound that the sister wives called home.

"You are free to go ma'am," said the police officer with the thick moustache and massive Ray-Ban sunglasses. But where exactly was Lemony free to go to? She had given the little money she had left to The Ministry Church of the Holy Order of the Eternally Burning Bush of Zion.

Now twenty-seven, Lemony was on track to become the first thirty-year-old woman who looked like a lemon. Estranged from her parents and soured by life, Lemony had officially gone from the spotlight to the street light, whoring herself out to any man who would have her. There were many men who would pay good money to sleep with a former child star, especially one as unique as the little lemon girl. Lemony, who had never been smart with money, squandered everything she earned. Most of it went towards supporting a heroin addiction she had picked up shortly after she started her life as a prostitute.

One day, the same network who had produced her reality television programme contacted her to find out if she was interested in filming a special episode of *What Ever Happened to That Person?* But Lemony's cell phone number just rang and rang. Earlier that day, she had injected herself with a lethal dose of what she thought was heroin but was in-fact weed killer. The network never got hold of the lemon woman.

A candlelight vigil was organised and held for Lemony by a few die-hard fans. Funds were raised and in her honour, a lemon tree was planted in the Braken Botanical Garden. You can still visit the tree today to observe a moment of silence and remember the cautionary tale of Lemony Sourpuss.

6
HAG

"There are those who warn against leaving doors and windows open after sunset. I, on the other hand, enjoy welcoming the night and the mystery it brings into my home. I worry not of the dangers. I have been safe here for hundreds of years and will remain so for hundreds more. What people don't know is, it is not I who need be afraid of what wanders into my cottage, but rather whatever wanders into my cottage need be afraid of me."

The old woman was hunched over a wood fire stove as she spoke in her dry voice. On the stovetop, a pot of something rancid was on the boil. None of Christian's senses were working properly. His vision was blurred from the foul smoke and steam emanating from the pot. His ears were ringing and his tongue had become a block of chalk in his mouth. Had he hit is head? The last thing he remembered was falling...and the spiders. Oh the spiders! He could still feel them crawling all over him. He attempted to shake them off, but it was no good. He had been bound tightly to a support beam in the cottage. He was not going anywhere.

"W-where am I?" he mumbled. The hunched figure turned away from the stove and hobbled towards him, coming out of the smog and into focus. She was hideous. Long, filthy tendrils of soot-coloured hair hung from her head like the roots of a dead tree. Her face was ancient, but not in the same way his grandmother's was. Grandmother's face was filled with wisdom and had the wrinkles of ten million smiles. This woman's face had twisted into something hideous after lifetimes of scowls and grimaces.

"You are with us, boy," she said through a mouth that contained only three, very rotten teeth. Her acrid breath flowed over Christian and hung in his nostrils.

"What do you want with me?" Christian asked, struggling to breathe. He didn't know if it was just the old woman's breath or if the restraints were getting tighter around his chest.

"My children need to feed," said the hag as her bony hand moved to expose her right breast. Or at least it was where the right breast on a normal woman would be. Instead, the crone displayed grey-green flesh, covered in irregular clusters of holes the size of coins. In each tightly-packed compartment something wriggled. It was like looking into a broken hornets' nest made of skin, with the larvae still squirming around inside. Christian's stomach churned and he was sick all over himself.

"They tell you stories about how children are quick and clever," the witch said, waving her twisted finger in Christian's face. "But I have news for you, children are not quick and clever. They are stupid and delicious."

She was right, Grandmother had told Christian many such stories. Thinking about them now, perhaps they were more warnings than stories. The children in those stories were clever indeed. Christian himself was clever, but he could see no way out of this.

"Someone will come looking for me," he said.

The hag let out a cackle. "They can look for you all they want, but they will not find you. Once I am done sucking the marrow from your bones I will use them to make ointments. Not a trace of you shall remain."

Surely someone was looking for him? How long had he been gone?

"I have ways of keeping you alive for a long time," cackled the hag, "as I devour you inch by scrumptious inch." She smacked her lips and salivated in anticipation. "It has been a long time since I had the good fortune of a child wandering into my woods."

In her bony hand she held a small bundle of dried out plants and sticks. A crooked smile wound its way around her worn-leather face as smoke started to rise from the bundle, followed by glowing embers. They danced in Christian's vision like fireflies as he grew heavy and weak with sleep. Christian tried his best to hold his breath for as long as he could but wisps of clove-scented smoke slithered their way into his lungs.

The crone came closer and waved the smoking stack of herbs right in front of Christian's face. "Sleep now scrumptious one," she croaked. "Let the darkness take you."

Suddenly the window, which was slightly ajar, was pushed open all the way by a breeze that blew into the cottage. On this breeze a whisper floated.

"Arrogant hag," the whisper rustled.

Was this the old woman's doing? Was the smoke he had

inhaled making him hear voices? But then, he saw the grin slide off her face and a look of unwanted surprise took its place. She'd heard it too.

"Who was that?" the crone shrieked, clearly startled. She spun around in circles trying to see who or what had skulked into her cottage. "Show yourself! Make yourself known!"

"We do not take orders from the likes of you," the whisper responded, as the breeze began to blow stronger, pushing the smog out through the chimney top and clearing the air. Christian's vision was now good enough to see the expression of concern on the old woman's ugly, twisted face. His mind was clearer too. The whisper continued, getting louder. "For too long you have resided in this hovel and gone unchecked. You have grown supercilious and forgetful of where your magic stems from."

The wind blew stronger, bending the branches of the trees against the cottage and causing them to scrape on the windows. The scratching branches made it sound like the residence was under siege by a hoard of gnawing rodents.

The hag dropped the burning sticks, fell to her knees and pleaded with the air around her. "Please!" she begged. "I am but a simple hedge witch! I have done no harm here."

"Lies!" the gust hissed, blowing a force so strong that the hag was knocked off her knees and onto her back. Both the windows and the door were blown off their hinges. Christian watched as the witch struggled to get up, but the wind had pinned her in place. Her filthy hair and ruined clothes caught in the whirl of the angry windstorm. "You are Phlegmhilde, Chewer of Children! Our roots run deep, witch! You cannot lie to us!"

The old woman was crying. Thick tears were running out

of her eyes and being blown across her face as she wailed. "Have mercy!" she squawked.

"There is no mercy for those who do not respect the divine balance," bellowed the wind, now louder than ever. The shadows of the trees grew longer as the branches crept through the window and across the rotting floorboards of the cottage. "You have taken too much from the world without giving back and for that you must pay with your wretched life!"

The hag let out a shriek as the branches and vines pounced on her, impaling her from all directions. A thick vine wound itself around her bloody torso and squeezed hard. The creatures living in her chest burst forth in a rupture of blood and pus, giant worms with human faces. They gave out the cries of new-borns as they hit the floor, where they writhed around.

Christian's restraints loosened as the last bit of life left the hag's eyes. He wriggled free and bolted for the now door-less exit of the cottage. The wind was still whipping around him and he found it difficult to keep his balance as he sprinted. Just before the threshold, his foot caught on one of the branches and he fell forward through the doorway.

He groaned as he lifted himself to his feet. The bright moonlight broke through the tree branches like silver shards of glass and the fresh air cleared his mind. His hands and knees had been badly grazed by the fall, but he was grateful to be out of danger. Drops of blood fell from the wounds and were quickly soaked up by the thirsty earth.

He stood amongst the fractured moonbeams, his heart still thumping in his chest. He looked around not knowing what to do next. He picked a direction to try follow out of the woods. It was awkward not having anyone to thank directly, but he thought that it was only right. "Thank you for saving me," he said to no one.

"Poor, naive child," the voice on the wind whispered back at him. It was the sound of a thousand sweet beckoning voices that murmured as one. In the shadows beyond the reach of the moon light, several pairs of glittering yellow eyes opened and looked at him like he was delicious. "We only saved you so that we may have you for ourselves."

Far away, a farmer had just finished helping one of his cows birth a healthy calf. As he walked from the cattle shed and back toward his cottage he heard a scream come from the woods. His spine shivered, his blood ran cold and he quickened his pace. He held his lantern high to guide his way and didn't look back. No matter how old he got, he was never fully comfortable in the dark, even on a bright night like this. Once back inside the safe embrace of his warm cottage he shut the door, shook his head and chuckled at himself. He blamed his grandmother for filling his head full of nonsense about what lurks in the shadows and lives in the woods.

7

THE LAST SISTER

"She really was kicking and screaming towards the end, wasn't she?" said Takurua, carefully weaving her coconut leaf basket together. Her hands were calloused and wrinkled. She no longer recognised them but they were still sturdy enough to do a good job. "She was calm until they reached the edge of the volcano."

The two frail women sat next to each other on the beach. Takurua continued to weave her basket, while Matariki watched the sun dip into the edge of the horizon, making the sea look like it was on fire. Behind them, smoke bellowed from the mouth of the volcano in the middle of the island.

"It was an utter disgrace if you ask me," Matariki said, bitterly. "Being chosen by the gods as a sacrificial virgin is a great honour and should be handled with dignity. My granddaughter Talia would have done a much better job."

"Some people say the louder the screams the better the gods can hear you," said Takurua, taking a break from her basket weaving. "It is said that if the gods really feel the suffering they do a better job of keeping the island safe from a volcanic disaster and provide us with a plentiful harvest season. Also, if Talia is still a virgin, then so am I."

"Some people's heads are filled with turtle dung," grumbled Matariki, choosing to ignore Takurua's reference to her granddaughter's much gossiped about sexual exploits with the young men (and even some women) of the island. "Do you remember when it was my last sister who was chosen? Now there was a girl who went to The Great Mourunake with honour. She didn't even shed a tear."

Takurua did remember the last of Matariki's sisters that went to the flames, for it was Takurua who put the crown of pearls on the girl's head and dressed her hair the day of the sacrifice. It was long ago but if she closed her eyes, Takurua could still feel the tortoise shell comb weaving through the girl's silky onyx hair. The girl might not have shed a tear but Takurua felt the fear in her, like stepping onto scorching beach sand in the middle of the day.

Takurua knew that Matariki liked to talk big about her family's devotion to the gods. Granted, she did have bragging rights, as no other family in the tribe had sacrificed as many virgins to The Great Mourunake as Matariki's. But not many of the other girls on the island clung to their virginity as fiercely as the ones from Matariki's family – except for Talia of course.

All the girls who had entered the time of the Blood Lily this season, and every season before this one, had many opportunities to lose their virginity, and Talia had not wasted a single one.

The Festival of the Bleeding Begonia, The Night of A Thousand Warthog Sausages and even the Peeling of the Ceremonial Banana. Talia actively participated in all of them with the stamina of a female lemur in heat. She was present front and centre, her legs as open as the tide is high. She flung her fanny to the wind with a reckless abandon unlike any Takurua had ever witnessed in her long life.

This was a fact that Matariki chose to overlook, even though she knew better than anyone the disaster that would befall the entire island if the tribe were to accidentally hurl a girl into the volcano who was not pure of punane.

Takurua looked over at her old friend, the sun had set now but she could still make out every wrinkle on Matariki's face in the silvery light of the full moon. She was crying – not excessively, but with dignity and maybe even a hint of pride. Takurua did not understand her friend's uncharacteristic display of emotion and was silent until the metaphorical coconut dropped.

"You encouraged Talia to lose her virginity, didn't you?"

"I didn't encourage her to lose it, I told her to utterly obliterate it," Matariki grunted, forcing her tears back with the determination of a stubborn old boar.

"Well, if that is the case then she definitely listened to you," said Takurua. "One might even accuse her of being an overachiever. The other day someone, I am not going to say who, told me that Talia has had so much sex if you were to blow into her vagina it would make the same sound as if you were to blow into a conch shell."

Takurua waited for laughter, but none came. Instead Matariki looked sombre. She knew that Matariki was the youngest of six sisters who were all offered to The Great Mourunake. She was the only one left and Takurua had often wondered why, but she knew better than to ask. Matariki had a tongue sharper than the business end of a fishing spear and she was not afraid to impale anyone with her words if they dared to offend her.

"My father groomed my sisters and me to be sacrificed from birth," said Matariki. "He told us over and over again what an honour it was to serve our island, our tribe and, most importantly, the gods. He told us it was our sacred duty as women to meet the flames. When my last sister was sacrificed I decided with everything inside of me that I would never be one of the girls thrown into that volcano. That night I made sure to lose my virginity. I don't even remember which one of the boys it was, it didn't matter as long as he got the job done. And he did. My father was mortified. He disowned me, but it was worth it. A few seasons later when I married Thanuki and fell pregnant, those nine months of waiting was the most terrifying time I have ever lived through."

Takurua had to fetch her bottom jaw from the sand. In all their seasons of friendship Matariki had never confided in her like this. She had always assumed that the sacrifice of Matariki's five sisters was a source of great pride for her and her family. She sat in shocked silence while her fellow geriatric tribeswoman continued her confession.

"Thanuki was a good man, and he knew how I felt about the sacrifices. He promised me that if we had a daughter he would never allow her to take part. I didn't trust him. The will of men is as brittle as coconut husk and their promises aren't worth iguana shit. I was afraid that he would give in to the pressures of the elder tribesmen. Then I gave birth to Kai and I had nothing to worry about. Let me tell you, I have never in my entire life been so elated to see a penis."

The stars reflected in Matariki's brown eyes as she reminisced. They held the wisdom of all her seasons but lacked the light milky glaze that so often overtakes the eyes of people when they reach old age.

"When Kai's wife gave birth to Talia I was petrified for that baby girl. I didn't think Kai was the type to let her follow the path of the sacrificial virgin. After all, I had raised him. Things are different when they are little, boys will believe anything their mothers tell them. But by then he was a man and I wasn't going to take any chances. From before Talia could even speak, I told her that when her time of the Blood Lily came she was to lose her virginity faster than a tree loses its leaves during a hurricane. Maybe I scared her and that is why she was so thorough in her endeavour but I refuse to apologise for it. She is still alive and probably pregnant with a baby of her own by now. Did you see her go at the Jubilee of the Blooming Pineapple Blossom? If that night didn't end in pregnancy for her then nothing will."

Matariki fell silent and continued to gaze at the stars. She had a slight grin on her face that did a bad job of hiding her pain from the loss of her sisters, the scorn of her father and the fear she had lived with her whole life.

Takurua regarded her old friend with new eyes. She felt shame for not seeing Matariki for who she truly was and instead just dismissing her as an overly religious zealot. Takurua had come from a less devout family and her father had passed over to the land of the dead when she was a small girl, long before her time of the Blood Lily. She barely remembered him and her mother had never pressured her into losing her virginity or remaining chaste to follow the path of the sacrificial virgin. Matariki had obviously not been so lucky. Takurua was now the one crying.

"You know what the worst part is?" said Matariki, looking over at Takurua for the first time since the conversation started. "They make us believe that we have a choice. With one face they tell us that we are free to take part in any deflowering ceremony, copulation carnival or fertility festival we choose. But there is another face, one they only use in private, when they sternly remind us that we have a duty to serve our people, our island and our gods."

Takurua let go of the basket she had started weaving what felt like an eternity ago and took hold of Matariki's hands. "All this time and I had no idea," she said, tears streaming down her face. She was not as graceful a crier as her friend. "I'm so sorry."

Matariki, not one to endure the luxury of emotional comfort for long, gently moved her hands away from under Takurua's. "It's all in the past now," she said, getting up and dusting the sand off her skirt. "And hopefully the future will be better for it."

"Change is the only constant, dear friend," said Takurua, trying to comfort Matariki while wiping her tears away with the back of her wrinkled hand. "Who knows, maybe one day someone will convince the tribe to start throwing men into the volcano instead."

Matariki let out a laugh from deep inside of her that Takurua was sure echoed all the way to the opposite side of the island. "That will be the day," chuckled Matariki. "This island will be engulfed in lava and ash before those men decide to launch one of their own into that bastard volcano."

"But we can dream," said Takurua, getting up to walk her friend home.

"Indeed we can," replied Matariki.

8

THE LAST DAYS OF GOMORRAH

A handful of low-level demons were playing pool in the corner while a few other fallen angels watched on from the bar. Purgatory was not the busiest I had ever seen it but not quiet either. The jukebox on the other side of the room glowed in all its neon glory. Someone had just put a Meatloaf song on, a guitar solo buzzed through the air. I looked up and saw the nymph come in from the rain, he was a little damp but not yet soaked. He looked around for a moment before making his way directly to the empty barstool beside me.

"This one taken?" he asked.

In all the years I had been coming to Purgatory I could count the number of nymphs I had seen here on one hand. Fallen angels and demons were among the most common of Purgatory's patrons, followed by a few fairies and the odd ghoul but very rarely a nymph. They were a forgotten relic of human belief, faded away into the recesses of time and reduced to nothing more than dusty myth. I sometimes wonder if it will be the same for the angels one day, when humanity adopts some new faith system. In a way I could already feel it happening. Each passing year I was beginning to feel less and less real.

"No," I responded. "It's yours if you want it."

Stories written about angels tell of how beautiful we are to behold but I can attest that the beauty of angels cannot hold a match to the beauty of nymphs. Nymphs hold the kind of allurement that hurts to look at but you can't tear your eyes away from. They radiate health and youth like fire radiates heat. It's an intoxicating splendour that has your mind run away with itself and fantasise a whirlwind romance. They are beguiling. Something that you can gaze upon and yearn for, but at the same time know you will never have. When this nymph lowered his rain-dampened hood, he was everything I expected. He looked around 20 years old with skin the colour of ripe olives and just as smooth. Thick waves of sun-kissed copper grew from the top of his head. The thing that caught my attention the most were his eyes. They were a grey blue, like the sea during a storm. I'd only ever seen eyes like that once before in my endless existence.

He laughed as he pulled the chair up and sat down next to me. "I'm used to being stared at, but not quite like you are staring at me right now."

My eyes darted to the floor and my cheeks grew hot. "I'm so sorry," I said. "I didn't mean to be rude. It's just that… never mind. I'm sorry, I'll go sit somewhere else and leave you in peace." I got up to leave but the nymph reached out and touched my forearm.

"Please don't go," he said gently. "I don't mind that you were staring. Like I said, I'm used to it. You just looked a little stunned is all."

I sat back down and the nymph retracted his arm. "You just look a lot like someone I met a very long time ago," I explained, not making eye contact, my cheeks still flushed.

"Well it must have been someone who terrified you," the nymph laughed again.

"Quite the opposite actually," I said.

The barman approached and the nymph ordered a glass of rosé. "Well, who was he?" he asked me.

"That is a difficult question to answer."

"I've got time," he said taking a sip of his wine. "I'm Aphros."

"Nice to meet you, Aphros. I'm Zazriel."

"You sound like one of the important ones," he said.

I scoffed. "Trust me, if I was one of the important ones, I would *not* be sitting here. The important ones rarely fuck up and when they do…"

"Then what?" asked the nymph.

"Let's just say, even God turns a blind eye when it comes to his favourite children."

I could see him burning to ask another question but the nymph didn't press any further. Everyone knows not to ask a fallen angel what he or she did to get booted out of Heaven. It would be like going up to a person and asking them what kind of underwear they had on.

"So, what brings you out tonight?" he asked, changing the subject.

"The same thing that brings every immortal supernatural outcast out," I said. "I had nothing better to do and I wanted to get drunk enough to forget who I am. What about you? I was under the impression that nymphs prefer human company."

"We prefer any company we can get our hands on," he said. "But personally, I just felt like a change of scenery. The humans struggle to keep up with us. Once you've spent a few hundred years partying with Dionysus, you could drink an elephant under the table. Also, if nymphs spend too much time around humans, they turn human. Humanity rubs off on us like a disease."

"I didn't know that," I said.

"I'm glad I could teach you something," he said. "So where did you meet him?"

"Who?" I asked, distracted.

The nymph laughed. "The one you say I remind you of."

"Gomorrah," I said.

The nymph's jaw fell open. "*The* Gomorrah?"

"Well there has only ever been one," I said.

"Please tell me everything." He turned in his barstool so that his whole body faced me.

"Why are you so excited about this?" I asked.

"Everyone knows the story," his sea storm eyes widened with interest as he spoke. "But it's not every day that you get to meet someone who was *actually* there. Were you there when you know…*it* happened?" He made an explosion sound with his mouth.

"The whole reason I was there was because of *it*," I said.

Aphros's eyes widened even further, and I could see the questions burning behind them.

"Stop looking at me like I'm some kind of war hero," I said, looking away from him. "I'm not."

"I'm sorry," he said and I could hear that he really was. "That kind of stuff just interests me."

I sighed. "Fuck it. I guess I don't have anything better to do so I might as well tell you."

"I'll buy you a drink," Aphros said, signalling the bar tender to refill my whiskey glass, making it my eighth for the night so far.

Angels – even fallen ones – like humans, don't possess the high alcohol tolerance of nymphs but this didn't stop me from picking the glass up and taking a sip.

"I arrived in Gomorrah three days before the burning sulphur rained down on the Cities of the Plains," I began the story, taking a cigarette out and lighting it. "I was sent to Gomorrah for the same reason Raphael, Michael and Gabriel were sent to Sodom. God had made a deal with Lot that if we could find ten good people the cities would be spared."

"I'm guessing you didn't." Aphros's wide eyes glistened in the low light of the bar.

"If those other three turds with wings had tried hard enough we would have. But they couldn't have been arsed."

"Why?" Aphros asked looking genuinely perplexed.

I laughed. "Do you think Lucifer is the only angel with daddy issues? He was just the only one brave enough to admit it and he caught so much shit none of us ever tried to pull that stunt again. But it didn't stop us from feeling a certain way. Angels don't like humans as much as humans like to think we do. They allow their inflated sense of self-importance to make them believe whatever makes them feel best about themselves. They talk about guardian angels, but I promise you there are more angels out there who would sooner push a human in front of a moving train than save them from one. Raphael, Michael and Gabriel didn't find any good humans in Sodom because they weren't looking for good humans. They were looking for any excuse they could find to light the fuse that blew Sodom, Gomorrah, Admah and Zeboim off the face of the planet."

Aphros was silent for a moment, absorbing what I had just told him. The rain battered on outside, clattering against the corrugated iron roof of the entrance. He took another sip of his wine before asking, "What happened in Gomorrah?"

"I did as I was instructed," I said stubbing out my cigarette. "I disguised myself as a weary traveller looking for a place to rest before I continued my journey. I was turned away a few times but because I was actually doing my fucking job – unlike the three pampered Princes of Heaven one city over – I carried on looking. It was about midday when I knocked on the door of a modest house, not far from the main market place. The door was answered by the human that you remind me of. He was warm and welcoming and upon hearing my story he invited me in immediately.

He was the 19-year-old son of a merchant. His name was Hadrian. His father was away on business but his mother and two little sisters greeted me just as warmly. They were good, some of the best humans I've ever come across. They gave me a room in their home for as long as I needed, plenty of food to eat and asked for nothing in return. When I offered to pay them they wouldn't take the coin. Hadrian offered to take me on a tour of the city the following day if my traveling schedule allowed for it. I accepted."

"How did you find it?" Aphros asked. "Was it as bad as the stories say it was? The most wicked city in all the world and all that?"

"Show me a city without parts that could be considered the wickedest places in the world," I said. "And besides, wickedness does not dwell in walls and streets but in the hearts of men."

Aphros said nothing, just stared at me like he was still waiting for me to answer his question.

"Some parts of the city were as bad as the stories say. I can't speak for the other three cities, but at least of Gomorrah this was true."

"You don't think what happened was right?" Aphros asked.

"Of course I don't!" I spat. "I never even got the chance to state my case for Gomorrah before Raphael, Michael and Gabriel gave the command. They got to save Lot and his family. What of Hadrian's family? Did they not also deserve to live? The cities were obliterated in a matter of hours. Thousands of lives destroyed, innocent and guilty. And it was all for what? So that Lot's wife could get turned into a stalagmite and Lot could run off to Zoar to be date raped by his own daughters? God *literally* forbid that men lay with men, but incest and rape is A-okay."

The whiskey was doing my talking for me now but I didn't care. Being drunk didn't make what I was saying any less true. I went quiet and Aphros just looked at me. "The world would have been exactly the same place it is today if those people had been allowed to live."

Aphros opened his mouth to speak but no words came out. His lips closed again while I watched him pluck up the courage to ask, "That was the reason you fell, wasn't it?"

"It was one reason on a very long list," I said, trying to simmer down and let him know I took no offense to the question." And just for the record, I didn't fall from Heaven. I jumped."

"I see," Aphros said, trying to be sympathetic.

"No," I said gently, not wanting to sound as harsh as I felt. "You don't see. I was there for all of it: Sodom and Gomorrah, The Great Flood, The Tower of Babel and the Ten Plagues. I don't particularly like humans, but that doesn't mean I want to watch them suffer. And I definitely don't like doing other people's dirty work, even God's. I understand that when a group of cities have more brothels than grocery stores you have a problem, but that doesn't mean that whores and the men who pay them are automatically bad and deserve to be blown to smithereens."

"It might just be a case of wrong place, wrong time," said Aphros. "They sound like the kind of people Dionysus would have loved to worship him."

I laughed at the thought. "More like wrong god, wrong place and wrong time." But the laughter faded from my throat.

"What's wrong?" Aphros asked.

"All of it," I said. "It's all wrong. The screams were the worst part. I remember them so well it's like it's still happening and sometimes I can't sleep at night. I often wonder about Hadrian's father. He was scheduled to return the day after the cataclysm. He expected to come home to his loving family and instead all he returned to was rubble and ash. I thought of waiting for him. I thought that I could at least explain what had happened. In the end, I didn't have the guts and that is something I have to live with every day of my endless existence."

"Forever is a long time to feel guilty," said Aphros. "Is that the reason you come here?"

"This is where all the fallen come to drink," I said. "Besides, what are you asking me for? You are here too."

"But I'm a minor and forgotten relic of the past," he said touching his chiselled smooth chest with both hands. "You used to be an angel of God."

"*Used to be,*" I said before downing the last mouthful of whiskey in my glass. "The humans seem to think that fallen angels only fell at the beginning, but what they don't know is that we fall all the time. Out of God's good graces and into the wilderness. I fought in the Great War of Heaven too, on what I thought was the right side."

"Do you think you picked the wrong side?" Aphros asked as his gazed turned to the pool-playing demons for a moment and then back at me.

My brow lowered and I shook my head. "I don't know about that. All I'm sure of now is that I want nothing to do with any of it. Good or evil, from where I sit it all looks pretty fucked up to me. It's all the same to be honest. The picture of good or evil is interpreted by the frame it's placed in, not the picture itself. Do you think Hitler thought he was doing evil things? He sure as Hell was but *he* didn't think so, I can guarantee you that! And it's the same for the two of them." I pointed up and then down to make it clear to the nymph who I was talking about.

Aphros nodded in agreement. "What was it like for you, when you fell? I mean jumped." He quickly corrected himself.

"It hurts like a motherfucker," I said. "You know you literally fall right? Through time and space and dimensions. It takes forever and you feel like you're being torn to pieces the whole time. But the thing I remember the most was the relief. I didn't have the weight of someone else's expectations on my wings anymore. I wouldn't have to dirty my hands for anyone ever again. The price I paid is that there isn't a place for me anymore. I'm not good enough for Heaven and not wicked enough for Hell, so I just roam the places in between. But I'm preaching to the choir here. You of all creatures know how that feels."

"Well I might have a place for you," said Aphros. "If you want to come home with me. I'll let you show me how they used to do it in Gomorrah." The nymph winked.

I got up slowly from my bar stool and ruffled my wings. "Only if you show me how to party like Dionysus."

"Deal," he said smiling and getting up from his stool.

Together we stepped out into the cold night air, fresh and cool like a new beginning. It had finally stopped raining.

9
THE STRAY ASTRONAUT

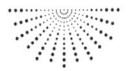

"Isn't he just the most adorable thing you've ever seen?" Moira asked, pointing at the ship's main view screen.

"Don't start Moira," Arnold warned. "It's probably riddled with diseases. We don't know where it's been."

"Oh, you don't have diseases, do you?" Moira cooed at the view screen. "Arnold, we have to take him home with us."

"Moira, you always do this! You can't just bring home every stray life form you find floating around in space. Look at its eyes, it looks totally feral."

"What is it, daddy?" asked Beth from the back seat.

Arnold ran a quick scan and checked the readings on the display, "Eew, it's a human."

"What's a human?" asked Beth.

"A lower life form with little to no intelligence," said Arnold. "I hear they also smell terrible."

"I also think it's cute!" said Beth.

"Its life signs are fading!" said Moira, rubbernecking over the readings. "It must have been floating out here for hours.

Look at all the debris, its ship was probably destroyed. We have to help it Arnold!

"It's a human being Moira!" said Arnold, "Do you have any idea how dangerous they are? Its ship probably came through an unstable worm hole, they are all over the place in this region of space. I'm surprised it's still alive. I'll just put it out of its misery." His finger hovered toward the controls for the plasma cannon.

"I don't care!" yelled Moira, smacking his hand away from the control panel. "All life has value. Now beam it on board immediately or it will be cold Glugian noodles from a can for you for a week and you can sleep on the couch."

"It's most likely gone loopy from travelling through the worm hole. One blast from the plasma cannon and this could all be over with."

"You will do no such thing!" Moira yelled, giving Arnold a sharp slap on his lap.

"Fine," said Arnold throwing all four of his arms up, "but then we are dropping it off at a shelter. That thing is not coming home with us."

Arnold rolled his eyes and begrudgingly put in the commands to lock on to the human before beaming it into the cargo hold of the ship. Arnold accessed the camera feed and displayed it in the corner of the main view screen. The human was on its knees. It threw off the crude breathing apparatus that covered its head and started taking massive breaths of air.

"The poor thing must be so frightened," said Moira.

"Aaaw," said Beth, "It's so ugly it's cute! Daddy, please can we keep him?" She looked at him, her eight beautiful black eyes glossed over with pleading and melted Arnold's third heart.

"Please Arnold!" Moira begged, giving him the same look as Beth.

"I'm not cleaning up after it or taking care of it." said Arnold caving in. "And if it gives so much as an ounce of trouble I will throw it into the atomizer."

"Yay!" yelled Beth throwing her arms around him. "Thank you, daddy!"

"You've done a good thing, Arnold," said Moira.

Arnold fired up the thrusters and put the ship on auto pilot before standing up. "I am going to go check on it. I want to make sure it's safe to take home. And remember what I said, any trouble and it gets atomized."

Arnold slithered into the elevator and pushed the button that would take him to the cargo hold. As the doors closed he thought how, out of all the creatures in the universe, he had the most compassionate ones for family members. He just wished they would have more compassion for his inner peace.

The lift doors opened to a wall of mist. "Unbelievable," said Arnold to himself. "The damn thing's been on the ship for five minutes and it's already ruptured a cooling pipe."

Arnold raised his plasma blaster and slithered forward cautiously into the mist. His eyes darted around looking for the human, and when that didn't work he resorted to clicking his mandibles and using his echolocation. The little bastard gave him the jump from behind. It had catapulted itself out of the mist and onto Arnold's back. Arnold used his two free arms to peel the human from his back and then held him at a distance. The human swung around in the air kicking and swiping at Arnold with its arms and legs. Arnold punched some commands into a wall panel in front of him to redirect the steam out of the cargo bay, clearing the air immediately. The human continued to thrash at him. "Seriously?" Arnold questioned, holding it up a little higher and taking a good look at it. "You are all four million years of evolution on your planet has to show for itself? Dominant species my left cloaca."

Arnold heard the doors of the elevator open behind him. He turned around to see both Moira and Beth slip into the cargo bay.

"Honey," called Moira, "Is everything okay?"

"I told you to stay on the bridge," said Arnold, still holding the thrashing human a safe distance away from himself. "Does no one in this family listen to me?"

"Daddy, don't hold him like that! You're hurting him!" Beth whined.

Arnold's jaw fell open. "Are you kidding me? This thing," he said shaking the alien at Beth, "attacked me!"

"I'm sure he was just afraid," said Moira. "He's probably never seen anything like us before."

Moira reached her arms out and gently took hold of the human. Arnold let go and it struggled against Moira for a second before calming down.

"How did you do that?" asked Beth.

"Your mother has a way with feral creatures," said Arnold.

"It's how I got your father to propose," said Moira as she rocked the human until it fell asleep in her arms.

"Is it a boy or a girl?" asked Beth.

"I have no idea, sweetie," said Arnold. "It's actually very difficult to tell with their species."

A loud creak came from the human's backside, followed by a vile smell.

"Oh, it's definitely male," said Moira fanning the stench away from her face. "No doubt about that now."

Beth giggled while covering her face, "It's going to be so cool to have a new pet!"

"Don't get too excited," said Arnold. "Remember your Bhaloovian budgie? We don't want a repeat of that incident."

Beth rolled all eight of her eyes, normally she would only roll three. "I was four years old, daddy," she said. "How was I supposed to know that the cage cleaner I was using was going to melt its flesh? What was I supposed to do?"

"Well, taking the thing out of the cage before spraying the cage with cleaner would have been a good start," said Arnold.

"I'll have you know that I was deeply traumatized by that experience," said Beth.

"Tell it to the carpet in your room, Beth," said Arnold. "It was so traumatized it had to be replaced."

"Daddy, stop!" yelled Beth.

"I'm traumatized too," said Arnold, "I can still remember the smell."

"Can we please not fight in front of the new family pet?" Moira asked. She was rocking the human in her arms when something caught her attention. "He's wounded, look at his neck." Moira turned to show Arnold three small puncture wounds on the human's neck just under his ear.

"It looks like a bite mark," said Beth.

Arnold pulled out his portable scanner and ran it over the wounds. "It's not a bite," said Arnold looking at the readings on the scanner. "At least not according to this. It's probably an injury he sustained while his ship was being torn to pieces by the worm hole."

"We'll get you all fixed up in no time," Moira coddled.

Arnold put the portable scanner back in his pocket. "I'll run a full body scan on it later," he said, "just to be on the safe side."

The human stirred in Moira's arms and slowly turned its head to look at Arnold. He was no expert on reading human emotions but he knew it had pure hatred in its eyes.

Ω

"Why didn't you just take the thing back to its own planet?" Ted asked, flipping burger patties on the grill. A week had passed since the family brought their new pet home. It stood on the window ledge glaring out at Arnold. He had been hesitant to invite Ted and Candy over for the Saturday barbeque, not knowing how the human would react to more strangers.

"Are you kidding?" Arnold said. "Earth is millions of light years and an unstable worm hole away. No one goes to Earth, you know that. Well none of the normal races capable of interstellar travel anyway. The Kremulans go there all the time."

"Aren't they the ones into all the butt stuff?" asked Ted. "Weirdos."

"And even if we did take it back to Earth," said Arnold, "another trip through an unstable worm hole would fry its brain even more than it already is. I ran scans on it right after we brought it home. Physically it was fine, except for a few bumps and cuts that correlate with a shipwreck. However, even by human standards, its neural pathways are a mess. Humans aren't made for the kind of space travel that one did. It's a miracle it even survived. If I took it back I'd be dropping a monster on Earth, and those creatures have enough problems as it is. Now instead I have to live with it in my house."

"Can't you just atomize it and be done?" Ted asked. "There'd be nothing left but a scorch mark."

"If Moira found out she would kill me," said Arnold. "She and Beth have become so attached to the damn thing. It never acts aggressively towards them. Look at what Moira made for it to wear."

They both looked over to the window where the human was glaring at them. It made eye contact with them while it scratched its groin and bared its teeth. Moira had created a pink lose-fitting jumpsuit for the human and topped it off with a collar and bell. The collar had cost more than what Arnold was prepared to pay for it but it came with a whole host of features like GPS tracking and a bio-readings monitor. Of all the features on the collar, Arnold was most grateful for the bell because it stopped the little bastard from carrying out its surprise sneak attacks.

"I'm telling you," said Arnold, "it's been a nightmare ever since Moira made me bring it onto the ship. It keeps trying to escape and when it isn't doing that, it's trying to kill me. Beth named it Frou-Frou."

"Well if you can't get rid of it," said Ted, "have you thought about poking around in its brain a little to see if you can make it more docile?"

"Ted, that's genius! I have all the equipment in the basement, it would probably only take a few minutes! But that's also so wrong! I could never."

"What's the point of having superior technology if we never use it?" Ted asked. "Also, the humans used to do it to each other all the time, they had a special name for it and everything."

"If Moira finds out that I lobotomized her pet she is gonna be pissed," said Arnold.

"She doesn't have to know," said Ted shrugging his shoulders. "If it starts to drool or goes squint you can just blame it on the human not being used to our planet's atmosphere."

"I'll mull it over but I still think it wouldn't be right," Arnold looked away from Ted and back at the window. The human was still eyeing him with an expression of great contempt and a shiver rattled all the way from the top of Arnold's arista to the tip of his tail. He flipped the idea over in his mind while Ted flipped the patties on the grill.

Ω

Arnold slithered out of bed the next morning and made his way to the bathroom to perform his morning ablutions. He opened the bedroom door to a scene reminiscent of a war zone. His eyes darted around the passage to the brown foul-smelling smears that adorned the walls and floor. Even the ceiling had not come out unscathed. Towards the end of the passage a section of wall paper had been torn away and a tile on the floor had been cracked. At the centre of the chaos sat the human with a look on its face that said, "Yes, I did all this and I would do it again." How was one small creature capable of so much defecation?

"Moira!" Arnold cried. "The human crapped in the passage again! It's the worst it's ever been this time!"

"Didn't you take him out to do his business last night?" Moira mumbled from the bed.

"Of course I did!" Arnold yelled, throwing his arms in the air with balled up fists.

"I'll clean it up in a minute," she yawned back at him. Arnold knew it would be a good hour before she would get up. His wife was a famous sleeper.

"That's it!" said Arnold, whipping his tale around the human and constricting hard. He lifted the human up and brought it to his mandibles. The human's eyes were bulging under the pressure. "The only reason I haven't eaten you yet is because I don't know where you've been!" Arnold threatened. "This ends now you little space demon."

Arnold slithered down to the basement and reached for the sedative emitter. He clipped the device to the human's neck and it immediately fell unconscious. He laid Frou-Frou on the work table and began running the appropriate scans. A hologram of what was going on in the human's brain and body projected itself in front of Arnold.

"A tweak here and an adjustment here," he said to himself while fiddling with the hormone producers and receptors in the human's brain.

Ten minutes later Arnold looked at his handy work and let out a contended sigh. "That should do it," he said before turning the equipment off and removing the sedative emitter from Frou-Frou's neck. The human being sat up and looked at Arnold with sleepy, but most importantly, calm eyes. "Yes!" said Arnold clicking his mandibles and punching the air. "I did it! No more crapping in the passage for you!" The human looked truly relaxed for the first time since Arnold had beamed him onto the ship.

Arnold lived the next few days in a peaceful bliss. He would no longer be attacked when he got home from work or when he got up in the middle of the night to use the toilet. The family didn't have to make sure to keep Frou-Frou inside at all times for fear of him running away because he no longer bolted for the door each time it was opened. Life was good, so good in fact that after a week of good behaviour Arnold even started warming up to the little guy. Arnold had in fact grown so fond of him that he finally allowed Frou-Frou to sleep at the foot of the bed between Moira and himself.

Almost two weeks passed and Arnold was lulled into thinking that the human problem was completely taken care of. It was on the fourteenth night after the procedure that Arnold awoke because of a weight pressing down on his thorax. He opened his eyes to Frou-Frou hunched over and foaming at the mouth. The human's pupils were dilated and his eyes were deranged as they glittered dangerously in the moonlight. The human growled before jumping forward and snapping its foamy jaws at Arnold's face. Arnold managed to swat Frou-Frou away just in time. The human hit the floor with a hollow thud and a jingle of the bell on the collar. It hissed at Arnold from the shadows and crawled under the bed.

Arnold flicked the switch on his bedside light and got out of the bed.

"What's going on?" Moira asked groggily.

"It's Frou-Frou," said Arnold, getting out of bed. "He tried to bite me."

"Frou-Frou would never!" said Moira sitting up. "He is a precious baby, probably just hungry."

"My darling wife," said Arnold. "Your ability to ignore historical evidence in defence of that menace never fails to astound me." All the feelings of resentment Arnold had held for the human came back to him in a flood of frustration.

"Where is he?" Moira asked looking around the room for her *precious baby*.

"He's under the bed," said Arnold. "I'm gonna try get him out. His mouth was foaming, I need to figure out what's going on with him."

Arnold laid down on the floor and peeked under the night frill of the bed. Sure enough the human's eyes shone back at Arnold, as angry as ever. "Pssss-pssss-psss," Arnold called out to Frou-Frou while reaching under the bed with two of his arms. He grazed the human with his fingertips before a sharp hot pain sliced across his lower right forearm. "Sonofanebula!" Arnold screamed and pulled his arms back from under the bed. Emerald blood was oozing from the holes in his forearm where the human had bitten him. He whipped the bed with his tail, startling the human and sending it bolting out the room. It ran towards the living room where Arnold remembered a window had been left ajar. Arnold ran after the human calling out for it. He reached the living room just in time to see it slip out the window. It had just enough time to spare to shoot Arnold one last dirty look before jumping off the window ledge and disappearing into the night.

Moira had followed him into the living room and switched the lights on. Arnold looked back at the trail of green blood he had left down the passage.

"We should get that bandaged up," said Moira reaching for Arnold's injured arm.

Arnold followed her down to the basement where Moira helped him nurse his wound. "I don't understand why Frou-Frou attacked you like that," she said, running a scan on the bite. "You must have given him a terrible fright."

"I am so sick of you defending that thing!" Arnold yelled. "Why can't you see it for the abomination it is?"

An alert popped up on the scanner's holographic display and beeped, drawing Moira's attention away from arguing with Arnold.

"Oh no," said Moira, looking over the readings of the alert.

"What is it?" Arnold asked.

"Your arm. It's picked up some kind of virus from the bite."

"That thing has infected me with a virus?" Arnold yelled, shuffling next to Moira to look at the display himself.

Moira started prepping a mixture of medicines into an injection capsule. "We should be able to stop it with this," she said. "Looks like we caught it just in time." She pushed the needle into his forearm with a little more force than Arnold thought necessary and injected the medicine.

Arnold's eyes ran over the data on the display about the virus. Moira was right, they had caught it just in time. "This is highly contagious and fatal if not treated immediately," he said. "We have to find that human or we are going to have an epidemic on our hands."

"This doesn't make any sense," said Moira, while dressing Arnold's wound and looking at the virus profile on the display. "We ran a full scan on him when we brought Frou-Frou home and we didn't find anything."

The guilt settled sharply into Arnold's shoulder blades when he put together what had happened. "Maybe the virus was lying dormant or something," he said. "Maybe he's not used to our planet's atmosphere."

There was no fooling Moira as she poured over the data the computer was collecting on the virus. "It was dormant," she said, "and would have stayed that way if Frou-Frou's serotonin levels had stayed normal. It leads me to believe that he was tampered with." Moira focused all her eyes on Arnold and they were all angry.

"Fine," Arnold confessed. "I may have done a little neural work on the human and made a few small adjustments to his serotonin production. I had to, Moira! That thing was a menace!"

"Well he is about to become a much bigger menace thanks to you! What were you thinking, performing brain surgery on the family pet?"

"It's no pet of mine! It's an evil alien from another planet."

"We have to find him," said Moira unlocking and opening the locker in the basement where they kept their more powerful ray guns and blasters. She picked up the dark matter rifle and checked its charge.

"Oh *now* you want to kill it?" He Asked.

"We have no choice, Arnold!" she yelled pointing at the display showing the data on the virus. "There's no reversing this. If we don't euthanize him then the virus will boil his brain in his skull! There's also no telling how many other people and animals he could infect. Grab a blaster and let's go!"

Arnold slithered over to the weapons locker and picked up the molecule destabiliser ray before following his wife. When they emerged from the basement Beth was standing at the door waiting for them.

"What's going on?" Beth asked, rubbing sleep from two of her eyes. "What was with all the noise?"

"Sweetie," said Moira placing a hand on Beth's shoulder, "Frou-Frou is very sick. Daddy and I need to go find him and put him out of his misery before he makes any other pets and their owners sick."

"Oh no," Beth moaned, making a face that just about broke all four of Arnold's hearts.

"I'm sorry, baby," said Moira. "But sometimes the right thing to do isn't always the easy thing."

Arnold wanted to say that the right thing to do would have been to leave that thing in space where they found it instead of bringing it home and giving it a collar.

"The collar!" said Arnold.

"What about it?" Moira asked.

"We can track Frou-Frou using that over-priced collar we got him," said Arnold, pressing buttons on his portable scanner and activating the tracking chip in Frou-Frou's collar. The display showed that the human was only a few blocks away. "Looks like we won't be responsible for the outbreak of a deadly disease after all."

"Let's go," said Moira unamused by Arnold's resourceful ingenuity.

"I want to come too!" said Beth.

"It's too dangerous sweetheart," said Arnold. "And you don't want to see, it will be too sad for you."

"Yes," Moira agreed in monotonous tone while giving

Arnold a dirty look. "If only there was a way all of this heartache could have been avoided."

A few moments later Arnold and Moira were in the streets of their neighbourhood tracking the human. The bio readings provided by the collar confirmed what they already knew. The virus was running rampant through Frou-Frou's body causing his temperature to spike and making him highly contagious.

"This virus is reproducing at an alarming rate," said Arnold, looking up from the readings on his scanner.

"What did you expect?" said Moira. "It's feeding on all the serotonin being produced by Frou-Frou's brain."

The couple continued their search, drawing closer to the human's location. Arnold was grouchy from being deprived of his sleep. He glanced at the time on the scanner, it was thor past squanch, an ungodly hour to be awake and roaming the street looking for a pet he didn't want in the first place.

"There are about a million things I would rather be doing right now," said Arnold. "That human has been nothing but an inconvenience."

"You don't think I'd rather be asleep like everyone else right now?" Moira retorted. "If you hadn't messed with things you had no business messing with then we wouldn't be in this position."

"You're one to talk," Arnold shot back, "as if insisting we pick up an alien life form, bring it home with us and call it a pet wasn't messing with the natural order of things!"

"I was trying to help it!" Moira said as loudly as she could without making too much noise.

"Well so was I!"

A clatter of trash pods falling over interrupted their argument. The sudden noise caused Moira to jump back and raise her dark matter rifle. The human emerged from behind one of the trash pods that was still standing. The virus was taking its toll on the human's body. Veins were bulging from its neck and its head was bleeding where it had ripped pieces of its scalp away. The flesh around its eyes was saggy and seeping yellow pus. It hissed at them through its foaming mouth. Arnold took aim and pulled the trigger on the molecule destabilizer ray. The shot of yellow light missed the human and hit one of the trash pods behind it, reducing it to dust. The human didn't run away like Arnold thought he would but instead stood its ground, hunched over and started growling.

"Daddy!" Arnold heard from behind him. "Don't hurt him!"

He turned to see his daughter slithering up the street. "Beth, go back to the house!" he shouted.

The human pounced into the air between Moira and Arnold, making a direct line toward Beth. In a moment of primal parental coordination both Arnold and Moira simultaneously raised their weapons and fired. Both shots hit the human at the same time – Arnold's in the head and Moira's in the stomach. The human violently exploded mid-air, coating all three family members in a thick layer of steaming black slime.

"Poor Frou-Frou!" cried Beth wiping the black sludge from her eyes.

"Well," said Arnold throwing the molecule destabiliser ray over his goo-drenched shoulder. "I think we've all learned a very valuable lesson here tonight."

"What did we learn?" Moira asked, putting her hands on

her hips and glaring at him. "Not to play God and mess around with the inner workings of another life form's brain?"

"No," said Arnold. "We learned not to pick up strays. Now if you'll excuse me, I need to go take a shower." Arnold turned to slither off and was quickly joined by the rest of his family. Beth on his right and Moira on his left.

"Do you think it would be okay if I got another Bhaloovian budgie?" Beth asked. "The house is going to feel awfully empty now that Frou-Frou is gone."

Arnold sighed, threw his arms over his daughter and pulled her closer, "I'll think about it."

As the family slithered away they didn't notice a large chunk of the black slime slowly dragging itself toward the entry of a storm water drain. Under the soft light of the planet's three moons, the slime slipped quietly into the sewer. The human's ship being sucked into the unstable wormhole had been its lucky break but landing on this planet as a stowaway inside the human it infected was the jackpot prize. Inside the damp sewer it would bide its time, slowly growing stronger until it was ready to carry out its primary directive. It had waited aeons, trapped inside the wormhole, it could wait a little longer.

10

DEATH AND THE SAD GIRL

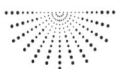

"We need to talk," said the tall dark figure at the foot of Amanda's bed.

She had awoken to him looming over her and was too afraid to scream. He spoke calmly and stood in a posture that did not suggest anything threatening or dangerous. He was still a strange creature with a scythe in her bedroom in the middle of the night and her heart was pounding in her throat. The stranger blended in well with the décor of her bedroom, like he was one with the darkness.

"Do you mind if I sit?" the creature asked pointing a skeletal finger at the edge of the bed. "I'm more comfortable when I'm sitting."

Still too scared to speak, she just nodded and the visitor sat down at the end of her bed. Amanda was sitting up with the sheets pulled all the way to her chin and her mouth open. His face emerged from the shadows to reveal that it was, in fact, just a skull. Amanda's brain started making connections, her fear had not subsided but she had managed to find her voice.

"A-are you the Grim Reaper?" she asked.

"That's me," he said. "In the...well I don't have flesh so I guess I am in the bone." He laughed at his own joke in a deep and warm chuckle.

"Am I dead?"

"No," he said, "but you keep wishing you were and that's a problem for me."

"What?" said Amanda, her fear slowly being replaced by confusion.

"You and I need to have a serious conversation," he continued. "All this morbid 'I want to die' bullshit needs to stop. Do you know how busy I am? I can't do my job with you nagging in my ear all the time. It's annoying. What makes your life so damn unbearable anyway?"

Amanda was no longer scared, she was annoyed. She turned to her bedside lamp and flipped the switch. Light sliced through the darkness and revealed her bedroom. It was just the way Amanda wanted it. Black and spooky. Her black bedding had been printed on in white to make it look like a Ouija board. Her black curtains, block out of course, draped luxuriously across the rail and had a print that made it look like a moonless midnight sky. Every inch of Amanda's space was drenched in glorious black. Mr Reaper actually looked like he fit right in. Like she had bought him from one of her favourite stores. The fact that he looked cool in her room didn't make her any less annoyed with him.

"You don't know anything about me," she scowled at him.

"You are sixteen years old," said the Reaper. "You don't know anything about yourself. Take the free advice of someone *much* older than you. You need to let go of all this anger and darkness. Life is meant to be lived. Every colour worn and celebrated."

"You wear all black," she rebutted, looking the Reaper up and down.

"Okay, first of all, I look badass. Second, I look this way because this is how humans have made me look. You guys chose this look for me. If it were up to me I would look like a friendly fat guy who wears Hawaiian t-shirts. And third, I know this isn't you. You love colour and foundation that actually matches your skin tone instead of that awful chalk paste you wear."

"You don't know what you are talking about," said Amanda. "This is all an extension of who I am and how I feel inside."

"Uh-huh?" said the Reaper, unconvinced.

"It is!" Amanda said, throwing a pillow at him which he dodged.

"Be honest. All of this is not a fashion statement for you, it's a shield and you know it. You don't want anyone to get to know you because you are scared that they won't like what they find. It's easier for you to scare people away. That is why you are lonely, that is why you are depressed, that is why you think you want to die and that is why you keep wasting my time. Stop calling out to me because you are wasting your time too. I've got news for you, your death won't be for a long time and I want to help you so that you don't spend all that time as miserable as what you are now."

"You are wrong," she said in defiance.

"Me? Wrong? Well excuse me," he said in mock shock. "I mean who am I but an immortal personification of a force of nature that is as old as life on this planet? What do I know about anything? I tell you what, if I am so wrong about you then why don't we just toss out all the hideous colourful girly stuff you keep under your bed?"

Amanda's mouth fell open.

The Reaper tapped the bottom of his scythe on the floor. The black night frill rustled and all Amanda's secret boxes slid out from under her bed, like they had been kicked out by something that lived down there.

"Would you look at that," the Reaper mused. "Turns out I do know a thing or two."

One of the boxes hit the Reaper's shoe. He reached into it and picked up a unicorn plush toy, it smiled at him and he turned to Amanda, "Very hard-core indeed." He squeezed it, it made a horse noise and told the Reaper it loved him.

"None of this proves anything you are saying about me," said Amanda. "Who do you think you are, just showing up here uninvited and lecturing me like this?"

"I didn't show up uninvited. You invited me here and you have been inviting me non-stop since you hit puberty. With your thoughts of razor blades and overdoses. And as far as who I think I am goes, I am the motherfucking Grim Reaper, baby!"

"But I want to die!" Amanda shouted.

"Stop bullshitting, little girl," he said. "You want to die about as much as I want to be having this conversation, which – to be honest – is not a hell of a lot. Do you really think that if I know what is going on under your bed I don't know what is going on in your heart and mind? Stop thinking about killing yourself because you don't really want it."

"And if I do it anyway?" Amanda asked, in the defiant and

antagonistic voice she liked to use on her parents when they argued.

"If you decide to be a jerk about it then this is how it's going to go down, I am not some costume party guest sitting here. I control the balance between life and death of everything on this planet. So go ahead, slit your wrists or swallow an entire pharmacy full of pills. If I don't want you, I don't have to take you. If you don't snap out of it and start enjoying your beautiful life then I swear that no matter what you do to yourself, I will keep you alive forever until you start enjoying it."

"You can't do that!" Amanda protested, but she quickly realised that he actually could. Her face softened and she looked away from the Reaper, her eyes filling with tears.

The Reaper scooted closer and placed his bony hand on her knee. "It's not so bad, little one. Give Life a chance and you will see there is a lot to live for."

"If Life is so great then why isn't he the one visiting me and trying to convince me to embrace him?"

The Reaper laughed, "I actually spoke to him about it. We agreed that you might respond better to me."

"Really?" she asked wiping away her tears.

"No," said the Reaper. "He was too busy and he wasn't the one you were annoying. But that doesn't make what I am saying any less true. If anything, a lecture on Life means more coming from Death."

"But you let lots of other people kill themselves," said Amanda.

"Not untrue and a fair point to make," he said. "Humans kill themselves for all sorts of reasons but you don't have any of those reasons and I am trying to make you see that. If I didn't think you were worth my time then I wouldn't have come all the way up here to see you."

"You said I was bugging you," Amanda said.

"You were. And I could have given you an aneurism or had you fall in front of a moving bus or just had you slip away in your sleep. It would have been easy but it wouldn't have been right."

"So what do I do?"

"I'm not sure," he said. "But I think you can start by wearing a different colour, on your body and on your life."

Amanda laughed. "I like purple. I am sure I still have something in purple."

"You have so much living left to do," he said. "If you only knew how many battlefields littered with the bodies of young people I have seen. So many people who wanted nothing more than to keep living. So many souls I have had to drag away kicking and screaming. They fought me every step of the way. And then there is you. An entire lifetime full of potential rolling over like a sack of potatoes. Check yourself and stop bugging me."

"So that's it then? You just came to deliver a message? No grand tour of what my life will look like if I carry on the way I am?"

"What the hell, child? This isn't a Charles Dickens novel. I don't have time to take you on a tour of your own bullshit. Death itself has appeared to you and told you that you need to get it together. This whole interaction has been a near Death experience for you. If that isn't enough then tough. Figure it out!"

The Reaper stood up and turned to leave but stopped and

turned back. "And one last thing. Stop wearing that awful make up. It makes you look like an anaemic raccoon."

He turned to leave again but something in one of Amanda's open boxes caught his eye.

"What is it?" she asked.

"Is that CD the Shrek sound track?"

Amanda nodded.

"Would you mind if I borrow it? I lost my copy."

"All yours," said Amanda.

He floated over to the box and retrieved the CD. "Thanks, kid." He said before fading away as mysteriously as he had arrived while humming the chorus to *All Star* by Smash Mouth.

Amanda was alone again. She sat in the quiet looking around at her black bedroom. "Maybe he is right," she eventually said to herself. "A little colour never killed anyone."

11
SWARM

"Did you hear what happened to Davidson and Harvey this afternoon?" Tess asked as she plopped down next to Chad in the police station break room. He handed her a fresh cup of coffee.

The sun had just set and all the day shift officers had left. The station was quiet, just the way Chad liked. Tess had brought a box of her famous homemade cookies. Chad loved it when Tess baked, she was great at it. She was a better baker than a police officer but he would never tell her that. If it weren't true she wouldn't be pushing papers and filing evidence in the station with him, she would be out in the field. Not that it mattered, Chad liked working with Tess. She was fun to be around and the two of them never ran out of things to talk about. Having her around was great, especially during the long night shifts.

The two officers were in charge of the evidence locker. It was tedious and uneventful work but it paid the bills and, in Chad's opinion, it was way better than being shot at (or God knows what else) out in the field.

"No, I only just got in," he said, eyeing Tess's box of cookies.

She opened the box and pushed it toward him. He took one out and bit into it. It was delicious as always, but apparently not as delicious as the gossip Tess was so eager to share with him.

"Harvey is dead and Davidson is still missing," she said.

"What?!" Chad spluttered, nearly choking on his cookie. "How?"

"That's not even the worst part," Tess whispered, "Harvey's body was total mush, the only way they could identify him was by running a DNA test. It was like he'd been totally pulverised or mashed up or something. The guy looked like a dropped bowl of red jelly. Dawn told me they had to scoop him off the road with a shovel."

Chad's mouth fell open. "What in the hell happened?"

"They're still trying to figure it out," Tess said, taking a sip of her coffee. "Bristow and O'Grady interrogated the only witness earlier today and you are not going to believe the story he is telling. Harvey and Davidson were patrolling the agricultural smallholdings when they pulled the witness over. While they were talking to the guy a second car comes up the road – an old-ass, beat up panel van from the 60s. Apparently it was rusted up and creepy looking. Harvey thought it suspicious so he pulled it over while Davidson handled the first guy." She dunked a cookie into her cup of coffee and took a bite. "I think I used too much sugar this time."

"Focus, Tess!" said Chad, trying to get her back on track. "The cookies are great, just finish telling me what happened."

"So the guy gets out the panel van and is a level 10

weirdo," Tess continued. "The tallest guy the witness said he has ever seen. He was dressed head to toe in leather – boots, jacket, the works. And he had a dirty scarf over half his face and a big brown fedora. The witness said he was standing a good six meters away and even he could smell him, said he stank of death." She paused to take another bite of her cookie. "Definitely too much sugar, you can't taste the chocolate chips properly. Maybe more salt next time."

"Oh my god, Tess!" said Chad. "Carry on with the story!"

"Oh, sorry," she said through a mouthful of cookie. "So the tall creepy guy had two big aggressive-ass dogs in the van with him. The witness said they looked rabid. The creepy guy left them in the van but when Davidson saw the dogs he told the witness to stay put as he went to give Harvey back up. They started asking the creepy guy questions about who he is and where he is going but he refused to answer. They decided to cuff him before asking what was in the back of the van, again he doesn't answer them. So they open the back of the van up and a swarm flies out."

"A swarm?" asked Harvey. "As in bees or wasps?"

"According to the witness," said Tess, "whatever it was a swarm of, they were bigger than bees or wasps and there were a butt-ton of them, enough to cast a massive shadow. You know, like the flies on Lake Malawi? I saw video about them once on Facebook, some trippy shit. You ever see that? I'm sure I tagged you."

"Tess, focus!"

"Shit, sorry! Sorry!" she apologized. "So this swarm flies around Harvey and Davidson and the next thing the witness knows, Harvey and Davidson are gone – like without a trace. The swarm then flies back into the van and the doors slam shut. The creepy guy then broke the cuffs off his wrists. The word the witness used was crumbled. The guy apparently crumbled the cuffs like…" she closed her fist around what was left of her cookie then opened her palm to show Chad. "It's the most unreal thing I've ever heard in my life."

"The witness sounds like he was tripping balls," said Chad. "There's no way this really happened, he was seeing shit."

"Maybe," said Tess dusting her palms off over a napkin. "But he's the only witness they have. They ran blood work on him. He tested negative for everything. He hadn't smoked so much as a dooby, never mind meth."

"Then he's a nutcase," said Chad. "He must have schizophrenia or something."

"No history of mental illness," said Tess. "He said the creepy guy then tipped his hat to him cowboy-style, jumped in the van and drove off. The witness used the police radio to call for help."

"This is fucking bizarre," said Chad, taking another cookie. "How did you even find all of this out so quickly?"

"Dawn called me on her way home this afternoon, she recorded the interrogation," Tess said. "And Davidson is still out there somewhere. They're apparently turning the agricultural smallholdings upside down looking for him but so far they haven't found a thing."

"You see, this is the reason I don't do field work," said Chad, waving half a cookie at Tess.

"Amen to that!" said Tess. "Nobody ever got abducted while filing evidence, never mind turned into mystery mince."

"I never liked Harvey and Davidson anyways," said Chad. "They were some of the biggest assholes in the station."

Tess shrugged, she knew he was right. Davidson and Harvey had crooked written all over them. Officers talk a lot and there was no denying that Harvey and Davidson had a bad reputation. What they lacked in likeability and popularity they made up for in fear and intimidation, not just among civilians but within the police force itself. Chad didn't feel bad in thinking the station was going to be a much more pleasant place without Harvey and Davidson.

"Wanna go see if the interrogation has been filed into evidence yet?" she asked. "We can watch it while we eat the rest of the cookies."

Chad smiled at his work bestie, "I thought you'd never ask."

Ω

ADAM DAVIDSON AWOKE NAKED and strapped to a steel table. The room was badly lit and smelled of rot and wet earth. The light grew brighter, just enough for him to make out that he was surrounded by hundreds of glass tanks of varying shapes and sizes. Inside the tanks were what he thought were insects. He strained his vision to get a closer look. He could make out the shapes and sounds of fluttering wings, the crawl of worms and the scuttle of beetles. There was something different about these insects. They all crawled closer to the glass walls of their tanks to get a better look at the naked newcomer bound to the cold slab.

That is when Adam saw it. They weren't insects at all. They were little people that were part insect – or insects that were part people. Some had two legs, two arms, a neck and head complete with pointy facial features and glowing blue eyes. Some had butterfly wings that sprouted from their backs. Others were lumpy, limbless worms with faces like melted cheese and sharp gnashing teeth. To his left was a tank full of shiny green beetle creatures that tapped on the glass with their mandibles to get his attention and then stuck out their tongues. They were making faces the way a small child would at monkeys in a zoo.

"Where the hell am I?" he asked the empty room.

"You are in my lepidopterarium," said a husky voice from the shadowy corner of the room. The man from the truck emerged out of the shadows. Adam recognised him by his height alone, he was now free of the dirty leather trench coat, grubby scarf and wide-brim fedora. Instead, he wore a blood-stained butcher's apron. The man's skin was black, leathery and pocked, like some of the corpses Adam had seen on the job. Homeless people that had died inside cardboard boxes under bridges and hoarders crushed to death by their own falling towers of junk. Bodies that had gone unfound for weeks, pitch black with decay. Adam shuddered against his restraints. Corpses don't move. Corpses don't talk. Corpses don't kidnap people, but this one did.

The whites of the corpse-man's eyes were bright as fresh paint, his irises and pupils in contrast were so dark you couldn't tell them apart. Two dark pits. A thicket of filthy grey hair grew over his skull the way fungi grows on rotting wood. Adam's mind was drawn back to dead homeless people, whose hair had the same matted look.

The living corpse drew nearer and placed a rolled up leather satchel down on the surgical tray to Adam's right. He undid the straps and rolled the satchel out, revealing a collection of rusty instruments that could only be used for torture.

"I am so glad you and your partner decided to pull me over today," said the corpse-man, running his black calloused hand over his collection of tools. He tapped a rust-clumped old fashioned hand drill with his long filthy fingernail.

"Who the fuck are you and why have you brought me here?" Adam demanded, but his words fell flat. Something was wrong with his throat. It prickled and tightened as he spoke.

"You may call me Sluagh. I'm a collector and breeder of rare and valuable creatures," said the corpse-man, not taking his dark eyes off the tools. "Are you familiar with tooth fairies? They are the cousins of the much larger and much more interesting bone fairies."

Adam didn't respond. The restraints had been pulled tightly over his arms, wrists, torso, legs and ankles. He knew that no matter how badly he wanted to move he wasn't going anywhere. He could still move his head a little and his gaze had been locked on to the tools sprawled out on the tray, until he noticed the silver sink and faucet at his feet. An icy sweat came over his naked body. He recognised that sink, any cop would. He was not strapped to a surgical table. This was an autopsy table, the kind people don't walk away from. A normal autopsy table wouldn't need restraints though, the one Adam was laying on had been modified for the living. For victims.

Adam's captor continued his lecture as if this was just another ordinary Wednesday afternoon. "The trouble is, bone fairies need a living human host to complete their life cycle. In a way this is a lucky day for you too. You get to have an experience few humans ever do. I would use my own body to host them but I haven't been human in quite some time. Unfortunately for you, the hosts of bone fairy larvae don't live very long after the incubation period."

"The what?" The words had to crawl their way out of the tight crack Adam's throat had turned into.

"Forgive me," said Sluagh putting his leathery palms together. "I forgot that you're a simpleton. Let me explain exactly what is going to happen to you so you don't feel left out. I'm going to take my little machine," he picked up the rusty old-fashioned hand drill and twisted the handle. It creaked and squeaked as the corroded gears spun and the drill bit whirled, "and I am going to drill your body full of little holes." He smiled, exposing a top row of serrated teeth, and put the drill back on the tray. "Then I am going to take my rare and beautiful bone fairy eggs and lay them inside your new holes." He licked his lips with his ash coloured tongue and quivered a little, like merely describing what he was about to do filled him with incredible excitement. "From there the eggs will hatch and mature into larvae. They will grow and expand inside your holes while your flesh heals over them. Once they mature they will burrow out of your skin and drop to floor where they will begin the pupa formation. Under the warm and humid conditions of my lepidopterarium, bone fairies will emerge from the pupae, ravenous for their first meal which will be your bones. Understand?"

"You are fucking crazy," Adam wheezed through his fear-tightened throat.

"The only kind of crazy I am is crazy-passionate about my art," scowled Sluagh, turning his attention back to his tools. "Part of the reason why bone fairies are so rare is because so few are willing to go through what it takes to breed them. A host must be found and sacrifices must be made. Long ago in the dark forests of Germany, there were entire religious sects of humans devoted to the bone fairies. They gave freely of their own to ensure the survival of a clearly more superior creature. Those people were dedicated, but they have long since died out. Be grateful and know that you are part of something so much bigger than yourself. You are helping to ensure the survival of an entire species!"

Adam wanted to scream. He wanted to yell every curse word in his vocabulary at this weirdo, but terror had gripped him too tightly and nothing would come out. Adam had been scared before, but not like this. His heartbeat pounded in his ears and his adrenalin-flushed muscles pulled tighter. He tried to struggle but he couldn't move. Something more than the restraints, more than the fear, was holding him in place, preventing his escape.

"What have you done to me?" He forced the words out of his mouth the way you force the very last bit of paste from a tube. Every syllable was a struggle.

"Just a little pixie venom to stop you from giving me trouble," said Sluagh. "It has the most amazing effect on the nervous system, the dose I gave you seems to be working well."

"You can't do this!" Adam wheezed, pushing the words from his strained throat.

"Tell me Officer Davidson," said Sluagh looking directly at Adam with those terrible dark eyes. "What's it like saying those words instead of having them said to you?"

How could this Sluagh freak know anything about Adam?

Let alone anything that Adam knew for a fact was not a matter of public record – mostly because Adam made sure it had never been recorded in the first place.

"Don't look so shocked Officer Davidson," said Sluagh lacing his long dead-man fingers together. His tar pit eyes widened, "My children whisper all sorts of things to me. If you listen carefully you might hear them too." He raised his large hand to his ear and fanned his fingers out. His eyes closed and his head tilted. The creatures inside the glass tanks got excited. The ones with wings beat them hard, while the ones without jumped up and down, clicking their mandibles. The room was filled with a cacophony of buzzing, crawling, crunching and fluttering. It got so loud Adam began to think it was coming from inside his head. "Ssssssshhhhh," hushed Sluagh. The little monsters in the tanks simmered into silence but left behind a ringing in Adam's ears. "My children have a lot to say about you Officer Davidson," said the man. "Bribery. Corruption. Brutality. Abuse of power. You have been a very busy man."

"You don't know a fucking thing about me!" Adam spat. The veins on his head and neck were throbbing. His ears were still ringing and his head was splitting. "Let me go!"

"I need you to understand something," said Sluagh leaning in closer to Adam's face, "you are not here because you are a piece of human garbage. You are here because like so many of your own unfortunate victims, you just happened to be in the wrong place at the wrong time."

This Sluagh, this *thing* that had kidnapped him was a lunatic. Adam didn't buy a word of this nonsense about bone fairies and pixie venom and what Sluagh thought he knew, but there was not a shadow of a doubt in Adam's mind that the madman was going to kill him.

"That's enough talk, Officer Davidson," said Sluagh. "It's time to get to work." The corpse man's hand floated over the tray of torture tools and came to rest on the hand drill. He lifted it with a firm grip and twisted the handle. The gears of the tool whirred and ground, sending the rusted drill bit at the end of the device into a fast spin. "Please feel free to try scream as loudly as you want, it so excites my children."

Sluagh didn't hesitate, immediately lowering his head he drove the head of the drill bit into Adam's right thigh. He twisted the handle fast and pushed down hard to make the fleshy hole bigger and deeper. Blood poured from the wound and spilled onto the cold autopsy table where it was then directed into the basin at Adam's feet. Adam felt every excruciating second of it but couldn't express a thing. He tried to scream but all that came out of his throat was the feeble squeak of a chew toy long past its prime. Adam wanted to shake his body, even if it would only cause the table to topple over. He would do anything to delay the pain, but no movement came to his muscles. He might as well have been a corpse on that table.

An eternity passed for Adam in that room while Sluagh carried out his macabre work. He drilled hole after hole into the policeman's body until Adam's flesh was riddled with bleeding cavities. He was awake for all of it. He had prayed to pass out but the sweet relief of falling unconscious never came. At one point he felt he was going to be sick, then at least he might choke on his vomit and die but his nausea subsided.

Finally the drilling stopped and Sluagh took a step back

to look upon his work with a sigh of accomplishment. Adam was drenched with blood and perspiration. "That wasn't so bad, was it Officer Davidson?" said Sluagh. Adam didn't respond. He just gurgled and wished to die.

Sluagh put the hand drill back down on the tray, bits of Adam's flesh still dangling from it, before he skulked into the shadowy edges of the room. He didn't go far. Adam could hear him rummaging around in the darkness before he returned with an old wooden box. He placed the box on the tray. It was just smaller than a shoe box and looked like it had been through hell. The sides and lid were chipped, scratched and stained.

"Find that thing at the bottom of an outhouse?" Adam wheezed. He wasn't even sure if Sluagh had heard him.

"You are very chirpy for a man that looks like Swiss cheese," said Sluagh. "This box is older and more magical than your puny brain can even fathom. Ancient spells have been placed on it that keep the bone fairy eggs in stasis until they are able to find a suitable host."

Adam wondered how his obituary would read. *Officer Adam Davidson, age 33, was murdered by a homeless serial killer who believes in fairies and magic.* He was going to die from sepsis at the hands of this madman.

Sluagh opened the box releasing a wave of miasma into the air that churned Adam's stomach. Inside was a collection of pearly white globes the size of large marbles. He removed a pair of tongs from the tool satchel and picked up one of the globes. He lifted it up into the gloomy light to admire it. In the light the milky globe became more opaque and inside the shadow of something small and snake-shaped twitched back and forth. "Isn't it beautiful?" Sluagh asked in awe. In one swift movement he lowered the egg towards the first hole he had drilled in Adam's thigh and slid the egg in with a squelch of bloodied flesh. Adam dry heaved in agony. This process was repeated over and over again until the box was completely emptied of its cargo.

"There my precious ones, grow strong for daddy," said Sluagh, placing the tongs back in the satchel. He then wandered off out of Adam's line of sight. He heard the squeak of small wheels being set in motion across the floor. Sluagh returned and came close enough to Adam to be in focus, he was wheeling a drip stand closer to the autopsy table. Under Sluagh's arm was a greasy old IV kit. He began to set the drip up with a precision Adam hadn't seen in even the most experienced paramedics. Sluagh's hands worked with a rapid grace, securing the roller clamp and drip chamber, attaching the tube and bleeding the air bubbles out. When the time came for the needle to enter Adam's forearm he didn't even feel a pinch. The man then secured the tube in place on Adam's skin with duct tape.

"What is that for?" Adam croaked, speaking had become almost impossible.

"It will take at least three weeks before my babies are ready to emerge," said the man. "We can't have you dying before then. We need to keep you alive and this is how we'll do it." Sluagh gave the IV bag a gentle pat with his open palm before floating away without giving Adam a second look.

Adam had become all but completely paralyzed, now a prisoner in his own parasite-infected body. There was no screaming, no jerking, only the hot tears that rolled down his face and onto the cold steel table.

Ω

THE WEEKS that followed were an ebb and flow of awaking in a burning pain and then passing out again. Adam had lost the concept of time and its passing. He dreamed of his loved ones, of his mother who would never be able to hold a proper funeral for him and who would then be alone in the world. He dreamed of Shirley. They were supposed to have a date the night Adam went missing. He dreamed of her auburn hair and the smell of her sweet perfume. You were supposed to wake up from nightmares, not wake up in one.

He was aware of the intruders growing inside him. They squirmed around their holes as they made a feast of Adam's withering body. They burrowed deeper and deeper all the while growing plumper until the day they hit bone. If he had been able to, Adam would have arched his back and screamed. The little bastards set his insides ablaze. He had to train himself not to look down at what his body was becoming. He was slowly rotting away while still alive. His wounds no longer oozed blood but a sick yellow pus that collected in the basin at the end of the table. His skin had dried to a wafer with a green undertone.

All the while Sluagh floated in and out of the room while his menagerie of freaky creatures watched Adam be slowly eaten alive from the inside. Sluagh's children, as he called them, pressed their ugly little faces against the glass of their tanks and ogled Adam with a morbid fascination. They reminded Adam of rubber-necking onlookers that would swarm murder scenes or car crashes. "Nothing to see hear," Adam wanted to say out of habit while waving them away. "Go about your business." Once a cop, always a cop.

Sluagh replenished the IV drip, monitored Adam's temperature and fed him icy water from a soup ladle. This process kept Adam on a flimsy tight rope between life and death. He was no longer a person but a living incubator for the monstrosities growing inside him. Every minute, there was less of Adam and more of them as they chomped away at his flesh, crawling closer to his vital organs.

Ω

"Your police friends are on their way," said Sluagh standing over Adam, adjusting his IV bag. "They finally figured out where to come looking for you, too late of course."

Adam wheezed at Sluagh and tried to make his face as aggressive-looking as possible but he was so tired, just the act of opening his eyes brought him pain.

"I needed to come check on you one last time before I depart," said Sluagh. "I needed to make sure that you would still be alive long enough for the larvae to emerge. It shouldn't be long now," he grinned in satisfaction, exposing his awful broken glass teeth.

Adam's eyes darted around the room. It had been stripped bare. The tanks and their grotesque inhabitants were gone. All that remained was Adam, the autopsy table and the drip stand.

Sluagh then addressed not Adam, but the parasites growing inside him. "My children," he cooed. "You have grown so strong!"

The growth of the vile creatures had caused Adams body to break out in welts the size of birthday balloons. They bulged out from all over his body, making him look and feel like a waterbed from hell. The only parts of him that weren't swollen were the ones under the restraints, they had instead been rubbed raw. The rest of Adam had swelled and stretched to the point where he could burst open at any moment. Adam had thought he would get used to the pain, but he had been wrong. Every second was agony. When he fell unconscious he no longer dreamed of escape or his loved ones, only of being delivered into the cold embrace of death.

Sluagh brought an open hand as close as possible to one of Adam's tumorous growths, without actually touching it. "The heat coming off of you is incredible! You were indeed a fine specimen, Officer Davidson. You've been an ideal host but it's now time to say goodbye."

Adam was confused and it must have shown on his face because as Sluagh turned to leave he hesitated and let out a deep chuckle.

"Oh don't worry, Officer Davidson," he said. "The bone fairy hatchlings will find their way to me, my precious children always do. They will only be in the pupa stage for a few hours. I just feel sorry for whoever is around the hatchlings when they emerge. Babies are always so ravenously hungry." Sluagh turned away again and left the room for the last time.

A door closed and locked in the distance and the movement began. It was a tingling sensation at first but it grew hotter until every inch of Adam's flesh was searing from the inside out. The bulbous sacks of dying flesh that were once his body began to move. The creatures were squirming around, getting ready to make their debut. With a sizzle and pop the head of a fat white maggot emerged from one of the tumours in a deluge of pus and black congealed blood. It's nub of a face wriggled in the air, taking in its first breath. Its slimy pale rugby ball body rippled and undulated until it finally emancipated itself from Adams body, falling to the floor with a wet slap. As soon as that was over the process started over again when the second-born made its appearance. So it went again and again until twelve larvae had freed themselves from underneath Adam's skin. Every second had brought with it a new level of suffering. He lay bound to the autopsy table with nothing for company but the sound of his slow, shallow breaths. His eyes floated around the room and he found himself missing the small creatures that would gawk at him.

He had no way of knowing how much time had passed between the birth of the first maggot and when he first heard the sirens. Help was finally on the way – not that it mattered. Sluagh and his collection were long gone and Adam knew he didn't have much longer to live. After weeks of suffering, the very last larva burst forth and crawled away. Adam Davidson exhaled for the last time and finally died.

Ω

"I'M THINKING OF GOING VEGAN," said Tess.

"Why on Earth would you want to do something like that?" asked Chad. "If you go vegan, you're gonna start doing things like using soy milk instead of cow's milk in your baking. The goodies just wouldn't taste the same. I won't stand for it."

Tonight Tess had brought a batch of her chocolate brownies to the station. They melted in Chad's mouth – the closest he had ever come to having a religious experience.

"I dunno," she said. "I saw a video on Facebook about how

they treat the animals and I don't think I feel right in participating in that cycle anymore. I'll share it with you so you can see what I mean."

Chad opened his mouth to respond but was interrupted by an evidence box being slammed down on the counter. Behind the box stood Officer Callum O'Grady. He was as grouchy as he was broad – and he was very broad. Chad didn't think O'Grady could look any more like an asshole, but he was proved wrong when O'Grady started sporting a thick moustache. It reminded Chad of the chimney sweep brushes from *Mary Poppins*, but without the dancing and cheer. Sharp and prickly, just like the grower's personality. A damp yellow toothpick protruded from O'Grady's mouth, he was rarely seen without one, like the venomous sting at the end of a scorpion's tail. In his five years at the station, Chad had seen O'Grady smile once and it was when one of the cleaning ladies slipped and fell on her ass.

"This one needs to be filed immediately," O'Grady barked. He didn't know how to say anything without sounding like a disgruntled gorilla suffering from a bad case of haemorrhoids. Chad considered O'Grady nothing more than an overgrown schoolyard bully who liked to throw his weight around and intimidate people.

"Is that what I think it is?" Tess asked, looking at the box, her hazel eyes wide.

"Stop asking stupid questions and just do your fucking job," O'Grady growled. "It needs to be picked up for lab work first thing in the morning so if you two knuckle heads could not fuck up and lose it for the next couple of hours, that'd be great. It's for the Davidson/Harvey case."

"Terrible what happened to them," said Tess, ignoring

O'Grady's sparkling interpersonal skills, picking up the box and putting it behind the counter.

"It's stupidity what got those fucktards killed," O'Grady grunted, chewing down hard on his toothpick. "But I'll be dammed if any evidence goes missing on our watch. The Chief has us busting our balls on this case, 24/7. So like I said, don't fuck this up or all our cocks will be on the block." He then eyed Tess up and down, "Including those of us who don't have cocks." He then strutted away like he had much better things to do than waste time talking to plebs like Tess and Chad.

Chad had turned red and once he knew O'Grady was out of earshot said, "The only time evidence ever gets lost is when cops like O'Grady, Davidson or Harvey make it go missing." He grabbed the relevant evidence forms and started filling them in.

"Did you hear what happened?" Tess asked.

"No," said Chad, looking up from the forms. "You know the only person I talk to here is you, so if you haven't told me about something then chances are pretty good I don't know yet."

"Dawn told me all about it on her way home." Tess jumped straight in. "They found Davidson late this afternoon, or rather what was left of him."

"Oh my god," said Chad, helping himself to his third brownie of the evening. He listened better with a mouthful of something delicious.

"It gets so much worse," Tess continued. "His body was tied to some kind of autopsy table, and by the look of it, something had eaten its way out of him."

"No way!" said Chad, between bites of his brownie. It was double chocolate fudge with a dusting of powdered sugar.

"Yeah," she said, "They tracked the panel van down through civilian reports. It led them to the basement of a building somewhere in the central business district. A good forty minutes away from the spot in the agricultural smallholdings where Davidson and Harvey were abducted."

"Did they catch they guy?" Chad asked.

"That is the worst part!" Tess said, "They didn't! That freak is still out there somewhere! A cop killer is on the loose!"

"More like Freaky, the Asshole Slayer, if you ask me," Chad joked. "Personally, I hope he kills O'Grady next and makes it three for three."

"Chad! Don't joke like that!" Tess said. "It could be one of us next!"

"I highly doubt that," said Chad finishing his brownie, licking his fingers clean and picking the evidence box up. He turned towards the inside of the locker and Tess followed him. The box was heavier than he thought it would be. "What's in here anyway?" The box felt warmer than all the others Chad had ever carried but he chose to say nothing. He didn't want to sound like he was losing it.

"Dawn told me it was all the evidence they found," said Tess. "Some kind of weird rugby ball-looking things, a whole bunch of them. No one knows what they are, that's why they are going straight to the lab in the morning for tests."

"Well, it will be safe here for now," said Chad finding some space on an eye-level shelf between two other evidence boxes. "Let's get the paper work done before we go on our break," he said before jerking his head hard towards the box and jumping back.

"What is it?" Tess asked looking stunned. "Is it a rat again? I'll die if it's a rat again!"

"It's nothing," Chad said, "I just could have sworn the box moved." He smiled at how silly he sounded. "It was probably just my imagination, I've been a little tired lately." They walked back towards the exit of the evidence locker while Chad wandered if he was lying to himself and Tess. Had the box moved?

"Are you okay?" Tess asked.

"My brain must have just been playing a trick on me," said Chad.

"I'm telling you," said Tess, "you should consider going vegan too. It's much better for your brain. There is scientific research, I read an article about it on Facebook."

12

THE FALSE PROPHET AND THE FALSE TEETH

"*I* am going to write a book," said Lynette, wiping a tear of laughter from her left eye and taking a drag of her cigarette. My mother, who was seated across from my aunt and smoking a cigarette of her own, was bouncing up and down with laughter. Tears welled up in her eyes making them look greener than normal. It was one of many Saturday afternoons spent visiting my aunt. We would drink kilolitres of coffee and consume the plethora of sweet and savoury treats she had baked during the week.

"What will you call it?" I asked.

"Die Wind Deur My Hol," she replied in Afrikaans and blew out a cloud of blue-grey smoke that hovered over the table where we were seated. The cloud lingered for a few seconds before disappearing. My aunt and mother cackled in chorus. I thought that The Wind Through My Asshole was a catchy title, but something inside of me felt it was unlikely the book would make it to Oprah's Book Club. There were many manic moments shared between us at that dining room table. On that particular Saturday afternoon, Lynette had just finished telling us a story that went something like this:

She used to be a typist at the local Police Station. It was part of her job to type up handwritten autopsy reports. It was the 90s and they still worked on typewriters back then. The handwritten reports would often be delivered to her desk with bits of blood and other unidentifiable bodily fluids splattered across the pages. The reports would read along the lines of, "The corpse was found after spending approximately 48 hours in the water." Gross stuff like that.

She admits that when she first started it was an icky job to do but, after a while, she got used to it. It was not uncommon for her to type a report about crabs having eaten away at some poor drowned bastard's face between taking bites of her polony sandwich. She felt it was like that with a lot of shitty things in life – you simply get used to them.

The men who worked in the morgue used to love messing with people. Lynette was the one who had to deliver the typed out reports back to the morgue because it freaked out the other two typists – Jackie and Carol – too much. Often when my aunt arrived at the morgue one of the coroners, a man named Bert, would lean against the big metal fridge where they keep all the dead people and ask her if she would like a cup of coffee. Bert was gross. A twig-like man who would slick his black hair back with Brylcreem. His teeth were so crooked he could eat an apple through a tennis racket. God ran out of skin when he made Bert and had to make do with the off-cuts from everyone else. He was blotchy and his skin was pulled as tight as the membrane of a drum over his face. Lynette loved coffee but only made the mistake of accepting a cup from Bert once.

"Coming right up," he said between his rodent teeth. "Do you take milk?"

"I do," she said.

Bert then opened one of the fridge doors and nestled between the blue-green feet of a corpse was a two-litre bottle of Clover.

Lynette took her coffee black for weeks after that.

Carol and Lynette used to get on like a squatter camp on fire but Jackie was a mythic bitch.

Jackie dressed like she had an epileptic fit inside a Hospice jumble bin every morning before coming to work. She consistently wore clothes that were ugly and did not match. Her dirt road hair was done up in a perm so tight it could pop a hubcap off a tire. Her porky face looked like what would happen if a cherub aged badly. She was a short woman who topped her look off with a pair of round tick-rimmed glasses and a wooden cross that she slung around her roly-poly neck. In my aunt's opinion, Jackie looked like a less glamorous version of Joey Haarhoff.

My aunt was a Christian woman and loved God but felt that was between her and him. The problem with Jackie was that she seemed to think she had a direct line to the Big Man himself. The Big Man was not to be confused with Jackie's husband Gerdus, who had the circumference of a dwarf planet and only wore khaki coloured clothing.

God would come to Jackie in her dreams. He would whisper to her from her coffee cup. He would converse with her in the bathroom. Jackie loved to tell Carol and Lynette all about her conversations with God.

"God told me that it hurts his heart when you eat so much chocolate cake, Lynette."

"Lynette, God told me that he really doesn't like it when you use the C-word."

"Oh Carol, God came to me last night and told me that if you don't stop wearing such short skirts he is going to have to send you to Hell when you die."

Lynette thought that Jackie may have had a point on this one but her relationship with God and whether or not you could see Carol's cookie depending on how hot the day was, was still none of Jackie's business.

Jackie can thank God that Carol and Lynette didn't kill her, but they didn't take her bullshit lying down either. One day, Jackie gave Carol a thirty-minute lecture on why the Smurf figurines on Carol's desk made God cry tears of blood.

"Smurfs represent stillborn babies and it makes God very sad that you choose to decorate your desk with poor stillborn babies that never even got a chance to be baptised. Did you know that all those stillborn babies are burning in Hell?"

Jackie was not aware that Carol had had a miscarriage a year before she came to work at the police station. Carol couldn't be alone in the office with Jackie after that and decided to come with Lynette to deliver the autopsy reports to the morgue. Jackie was such a bitch that her co-workers would rather spend time with dead people...and Bert.

Carol cried all the way to the morgue and it made Lynette want to punch Jackie in her C-word.

When Carol and Lynette stepped inside the morgue Bert offered them coffee. They said no thank you.

The morgue was within walking distance of the police station, but in order to get there and back again Carol and Lynette had to cross over several busy streets. They were in no rush to get back to the office and Her Holy Lady of Divine Bullshit, so they took their time.

"What the fuck is that?" said Carol in a disgusted shrill and pointed towards something fleshy in the gutter of the street.

Lynette stood over the fleshy thing and leaned in to get a closer look. "Holy shit! It's a set of false teeth!" They were the nastiest most grit-incrusted dentures she had ever seen. She looked over to Carol who had a naughty grin spread across her face.

"I have an idea," she said.

They cleaned them. Scrubbed them. Soaked them in bleach for 24 hours. They didn't want to kill Jackie or give her a nasty disease, they just wanted to scare her, make her shit her pants at the most.

Jackie was one of those busy-body Jack-in-the-Box kind of colleagues. She was often away from her seat. It was easy for Carol to make her way over to Jackie's desk and carefully slip the top row of dentures into the sandwich that Jackie was about to enjoy for lunch. She was fastidious in her re-arrangement of the lettuce and tomato to conceal the false teeth from sight. Once she was done, she darted back to her desk.

Carol and Lynette waited for the moment of truth. That self-righteous bible-basher was about to get a mouthful to end all mouthfuls. On her return, Jackie waddled over to her desk and sat down. She picked up her sandwich, closed her eyes and took a large bite. Lynette could hear the lettuce crunch and the tomato squish from her desk as she struggled to keep her composure. She clamped her hands over her mouth, tears streaming out her eyes. She looked over at

Carol who was stone cold, working away as if she had no idea what was going on. Jackie let out a scream that made Bert all the way over at the morgue look up. She threw her sandwich across the room, jumped up from her desk and bolted down the passage towards the bathroom.

Carol and Lynette were dying with laughter. They clutched their sides crying and cackling like two witches at full moon. Jackie did not make it to the bathroom before projectile vomiting all the way down the passage. When their manager caught on to what happened he forced Carol and Lynette to clean Jackie's puke. It was gross but it was worth it because, after that day, Jackie never said a word to Lynette or Carol ever again.

13

KEEPING GEOFFREY'S HEAD

Geoffrey's very presence would annoy me to the point of screaming, but Slurp (that is what I call it now) is actually quite pleasant to have around. It is like a friendly dog or a small child with a diminished capacity. I call it Slurp because that is one of the noises it makes when I let it out of the box every now and again. It gnaws at the feet of my bed with its gums.

Geoffrey was never meant to be one of my test subjects. It just sort of...happened. I was not trying to incite a zombie apocalypse or anything like that. And, before you get excited, I never did. I have seen enough of those movies to know better. Which is why, shortly after I decided to keep Slurp, I pulled all his teeth out with the pliers from my beading kit. I can still feel the dainty metallic pinchers clamping tightly onto his incisors. I might take up dentistry as a new hobby. I still don't know if what I did to Geoffrey is contagious, but I couldn't be too careful. Also, this is Geoffrey we are talking about and I am sure that he would be just as determined to make me miserable in un-death as he was in life.

I was trying to stabilise an artificial chemical-protein compound that would help regenerate damaged tissue. It would have assisted burn victims with quicker recovery and would eliminate the need for painful skin grafts. I know I am just a housewife but I am allowed to have hobbies. Also, what is the point of having a degree in biochemical engineering if all you are going to do is bake chocolate chip muffins all day? Even if they are the most delicious muffins in the world and always outsell all the other goods at the community bake sale. I can still feel Mary Osborne's look of jealousy and disgust burning into the back of my skull as my muffins outsold her dry and dusty apple upside-down cake.

I was running tests on a few small animals that I kept in the basement but I was not getting results. I needed a human. Geoffrey probably thought that I spent all my time down there scrapbooking – but then again, Geoffrey never did much thinking. On the night it happened, I emerged from the basement feeling defeated and made my way into the TV room. There he was, the blob of a man I had married. The look on his face was expressionless, the dull blue light from the television set cast shadows over his face in all the wrong ways. I could have sworn that he was drooling a little.

Every day he kept the same routine. He would arrive home from his job as an actuary, dump his briefcase on the mahogany dining room table and – completely ignoring my as-close-to-perfect-as-God flower arrangements – strip down to his sweat-stained underwear, vest and socks, plonk himself down on the couch and rot in front of that infernal screen. He is doing a different kind of rotting now but he was a zombie long before I interfered with him. He would always take his dinner in front of the television too. This alone was a slap in my face. The culinary art that I create is to be savoured and enjoyed, not shovelled down one's greasy pie-hole while Duck Dynasty invades every nook and cranny of the room.

I took a seat on the couch next to the sofa Geoffrey was sitting on. His plate was clean. I had made Chicken Cordon Bleu that night, with fresh steamed broccoli, sweet corn and golden roasted potatoes. For dessert, jumbo Crème Brûlée.

"Did you enjoy your dinner darling?" I asked, trying to sound as pleasant as possible.

"Yeah," Geoffrey grunted not taking his eyes off the television screen, "it was alright."

I looked at him with wide, furious eyes and I could feel a vein bulge in my right temple. Of all the words he could have used to describe the meal that I had prepared for him, he chose "alright". I had eaten the same meal that night. The chicken was tender and melted apart with the slightest touch of my fork. The bacon and mozzarella cheese stuffing was steaming and delicious. The broccoli was so crisp that I could taste the sunlight that went into growing it. The sweet corn – NOT from a can – was creamy and the potatoes were roasted to perfection, crunchy outsides and soft, fluffy insides. The Crème Brûlée, which I happen to know is Geoffrey's favourite, was amazing. I had to break out my butane blow torch to make that dessert for God's sake! But according to my Neanderthal of a husband it was just "alright".

That is when the thought crept into my mind, like a snake slithering its way across the hot desert sand. What harm could it possibly do? After all, I had seen no adverse effects with my animal test subjects. At worst, it would make him as nauseous as the very sight of him made me. I am not an impulsive woman but something came over me that night. I ran down to the basement and filled a syringe with my chemical compound. After the events of that warm summer evening I decided to name it *Resurrex*.

The thick amber fluid filled the syringe, I lopped back upstairs to Geoffrey and stood behind him. He took no notice of me. I leaned in as if I were about to caress him. I took a moment to look at his short fat neck, the result of over indulging in convenience store pies and soft drinks.

I hated him. I hated him in general but in that moment I hated him with something inside of me that, up until then, I had been unaware of. It burned in me like hellfire, consuming everything in its path. My logic, my common sense, the love that I had once felt for him was devoured by the inferno of hatred and spite I had towards my husband. In a viper-fast move of my arm I jabbed the needle into his neck. I didn't care about which vein to hit and where to hit it; I just let the thin metal fly and land where it may, then I pushed down hard on the plunger of the syringe.

Before the words "what the fuck, Marian" could even escape his lips, he dropped down dead to the floor! I looked at him and then at the TV remote resting on the arm of the couch. I picked up the remote and turned the TV off. Beautiful, sweet silence. I considered sitting down on the couch where Geoffrey had been sitting before I accidentally-on-purpose killed him, but it would still be warm with his body heat and that would just be wrong. I picked a spot on a different couch and stared at my husband's fresh corpse.

Obviously my calculations were a little off.

I was more upset about the fact that my compound hadn't worked than the fact that I had just killed Geoffrey. I sat in silence for a long while wondering where I had gone wrong. You can imagine my shock when he grunted and started moving again. "He is going to be so angry," I thought, which made me laugh until I noticed that, while he was indeed moving, there was no one home. I had turned my useless, filthy, schmuck of a husband into a zombie.

I am a woman of many talents and one of them is that I am very good at cleaning up messes. I was concerned that Geoffrey was too big of a mess from me to handle but, then again, I like a challenge. Once I realised that he was no longer amongst the living but not quite amongst the dead either, I ran to the kitchen, grabbed my George Foreman and thwacked Geoffrey hard over the head with it, leaving him unconscious once more.

I stood with the electric grill dangling from my right hand. "Damn that felt good," I thought to myself. "I've wanted to do that for ages!" I wanted to roll Geoffrey's body up inside the living room rug like you see in the movies, but it is Persian and I pride myself on keeping it in pristine condition. I didn't want to risk Geoffrey waking up and attacking me so I tied his arms and legs together with cable ties from the garage before I started the exodus to the basement. The best way I could describe Geoffrey's body type is that of an elderly, obese elephant seal so it was a lengthy haul indeed.

By the time I got to the door of the basement I was too tired and out of breath to care. With the last of my strength I gave a final heave and pushed the undead good-for-nothing down the stairs. And before you suggest that I have no respect for the dead, remember that we are talking about a man who would clean the grit from underneath his finger nails at the dinner table with a tooth pick, and then use the same toothpick to loosen the remnants of his meal from between his large teeth. We are talking about the same man who would squeeze his zits out against my freshly polished bathroom mirror and then leave without cleaning up or washing his hands. In life or in death – or in undeath – I would never have respect for Geoffrey.

His corpse hit the stairs on the way down with a thud each time he made impact, until he came to rest in a contorted pile on the floor. I know nothing about how to get rid of a dead body but I have carved enough roasts, filleted enough fish and deboned enough chickens. I retrieved my electric carving knife, meat hammer, food processor, power peeler and, just for fun, the nut cracker too.

There, between my lab equipment and scrap booking collection I heaved Geoffrey onto my craft table and set to work.

You don't really know how difficult it is to cut up a dead body until you have actually done it. It turned out that Geoffrey's flesh was just as stubborn and unpleasant to deal with as his personality.

God, it stank. I started at his feet and made my way up. I don't know how long it took but I do know that by the time I had neatly sliced, diced, chopped and drained my husband the sun was peeping through the small rectangular window in the basement. Spatters of blood covered me. My sunflower yellow day dress was ruined. I would later burn the dress in the back yard.

I stood amongst the buckets of blood, bone, fat and skin,

happy with a job well done. I made a mental note to later thank the Home Shopping Network in an email for producing such good quality products – money well spent.

I packed all the pieces of Geoffrey into Ziplock bags and then packed the bags neatly into my industrial-sized freezer. I stored them there for safe keeping until I was able to dispose of them, which I did bit by bit. Every day, I would put one bag in the trash which the garbage men would then take away, never to be seen again.

It was as simple as that – that is until the time came for me to decide what to do with the last piece of Geoffrey: his head. When I turned to pick up the head, its eyelids flung open and it gazed at me. For a moment, the hardness in my heart towards Geoffrey faltered. I felt like a bad joke; what is worse than killing your husband? Killing your husband and holding onto his zombified head as a keepsake. The head gurgled at me and the blue eyes drifted in different directions. The right eye gazed left, while the left eye stared at the floor. This softened my heart. I kept the head and three days later I christened it Slurp.

$$\Omega$$

I MADE pizza tonight as a treat. I made it from scratch of course; I don't tolerate that store bought pizza base. I just figure if one is going to do something then you shouldn't take short cuts. It's lazy. The base is cooked beautifully, it is light and crunchy and the toppings are well selected. Pizza is Slurp's favourite. I love watching him enjoy it. I sit at the edge of the bed tearing at pieces of pepperoni and toss them into the box. I don't know where he puts it all as he has no stomach but he gobbles up every little bite, even the crusts. I look down at him as he gurgles and burps and I cannot understand how he has better table manners than Geoffrey ever did.

Over the past few weeks he has begun to decompose. His flesh has turned a green-yellow colour and he smells horrific, but a few short bursts of fabric freshener take the smell away immediately. I know that I can't hold on to him forever, but I'm enjoying the company for now. I was thinking of getting a dog after I eventually get rid of Slurp but it just won't be the same.

The day the police came round I played dumb. I told them Geoffrey had gone for a walk the night he "went missing" and never returned. It's a good thing they don't know Geoffrey was too lazy to stand up from the couch if he didn't have to, never mind walk anywhere. I reported Geoffrey missing myself as I figured I would be the first one to notice his absence so it made sense.

"If there is anything else you can remember about that night ma'am, you need to tell me. Any detail, no matter how small, could make a difference to the investigation," said the officer as he leaned against my kitchen counter top. His posture suggested that he was bored. I noticed that there was a pale mark around his left ring finger. He must be a new divorcé, which would explain why his shirt looked like it had been ironed by a monkey with no hands. He looked young to already be married and divorced, but I didn't dwell on it. He came in alone, I noticed that his partner remained in the police van, unwilling to brave the simmering heat, opting to stay in the car where it was air-conditioned.

"Would you like a drink to cool you down, officer?" I

offered, my hands shaking as I grabbed hold of the glass pitcher. I was not shaking out of nerves or guilt but out of sheer exhaustion. I had not slept at all. Between disposing of Geoffrey, getting rid of evidence and working on the breakthrough in my compound there had been no time for sleep. I was starting to feel like a zombie myself. I looked like hell but that only made my whole 'beside herself with worry wife' façade more believable.

I gave the lemonade a stir, the metal spoon clinking against the sides of the pitcher.

The heat that day was intense and I could see the beads of sweat that had formed under the brim of the officer's hat. He wiped his forehead with a handkerchief produced from his breast pocket.

"That would be much appreciated ma'am."

I poured the officer a tall glass of my special homemade lemonade and watched his Adam's Apple slide up and down his throat as he gulped down every last drop.

"Aaah," he sighed. "Ma'am that must be the best damn lemonade I have ever had."

"That is very kind of you," I said. I wanted him out of the house so I could finally get some rest. People never see things from a murderer's perspective so let me tell you: murder is highly stressful and exhausting. I needed at least a massage and a facial, probably a manicure too – getting Geoffrey out from under my nails had ruined them.

"I am distraught officer, I don't know what I would do without my Geoffrey," I lied. "Please tell me that you will find him."

"We will do our best ma'am," he said flipping his note

book closed and sliding it into his pocket. "We will call you the moment we find anything."

'I won't hold my breath,' I thought to myself but out loud I simply thanked him, ushered him out and closed the door tightly behind him.

I am just the simple housewife whose husband was missing, presumed dead. How could I be suspected of anything? Even if they had done a search of the house they would not have found any evidence. Most of the bags containing Geoffrey went with the garbage man that morning and the rest went the next day. I made sure to swab down every surface and tool with industrial-grade bleach. I wiped every trace of another human being clean off the face of the Earth. He is gone forever and I will forever be relieved. Sometimes the best things in life happen to us by accident, after we decide to take charge.

Ω

I NEVER GIVE a second thought to what I will do without Geoffrey, because I was never really with him in the first place, at least not for the last few years of our marriage. We have enough money saved and invested, so I will not have to worry about supporting myself and I am sure his life insurance policies will pay out eventually. I will do what I have always done: cook, clean, bake, host Bridge with my friends every other Tuesday, enter bake sales and, of course, I will always have my hobbies.

If the police had found Slurp I would have just told them that he is a special effect Halloween decoration that I have been working on, one of my many hobbies. They would be uncomfortable for a second but then they would congratulate me on a job well done, put the lid back on the box and go about their business. Besides, as with most things in life, I don't think anyone would believe me if I told the truth anyway.

14
THE TOWER

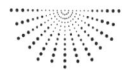

It started with a rumour. It circulated amongst the peasants in the market places until, like an invasive vine, it made its way up to the halls of the palace where it came to rest on the ears of the royal court. By the time it reached Prince Tristan the entire kingdom was abuzz with talk.

A fair maiden had been trapped in a tall tower, guarded by an evil witch. The maiden's golden hair had grown long and strong and she would let it down for any man brave enough to try rescue her. The window through which she would lower her trusses was the only entrance to the tower. The maiden however was not the only prize. It was also said the witch hoarded riches beyond imagination in the tower. Enough gold and jewels to make a man a king or to make a king an emperor.

Prince Tristan could not resist the temptation of glory. A quest like this was just the thing he was looking for to prove his worth to himself and, more importantly, get out from under the thumb of his father the king.

While Tristan knew many had set out to slay the witch, rescue the maiden and claim the treasure, prince and pauper alike, they were never heard from again. Their fate would not be his. After all, he was the crown Prince of Thraxia.

Tristan sat at the head of the table in his private court; a collection of individuals he liked to keep around to entertain and advise him. The king did not approve of the company his son kept but the prince found his collection of riffraff and whores incredibly useful. They had earned a nickname from the real royal court: The Court of Repugnance. Tristan had no time for royal gossip, he wanted to stay in touch with the dark underbelly of the kingdom and if he had to dine with whores and murderers to do it then he would. Tristan preferred his Court of Repugnance over the real courtiers anyway. They were real people who understood how the real world worked, not pampered palace brats whose biggest concerns were how much to powder their fat faces or how to get their wigs as high as possible. They bored him to revulsion and worse yet, were useless in the bedroom.

Tristan had not uttered a word to anyone about the maiden, the witch and the tower. Instead, he listened while The Court of Repugnance passionately discussed the subject over many glasses of wine and an elaborate meal. They dined in one of the deepest forgotten recesses of the palace. It was more dungeon cave than banquet hall but they would not be disturbed. He had christened their meeting place, the Chamber of the Wretched.

Tristan would smuggle his band of misfits to the chamber through secret passages in the palace he had committed to memory as a child. There they would discuss matters of the kingdom and share secrets in the dim candle light while they feasted, drank and fornicated themselves sick.

"Prince Tristan should free the maiden!" shouted Ortho, the Executioner, thrusting a goblet of wine in the air, spilling half of it on Boo-Boo the dwarf, who served as the court fool.

"Yes!" Sredence the Shadow agreed. "His majesty is perfect for the job and success would bring great honour to your name!"

This is exactly what Tristan had been waiting for. It wasn't enough for him to outright take the challenge on. He wanted his court to lay it down in front of him. He wanted to make them think it was their idea. It made for more interesting songs for the bards to sing and it made Tristan look brave instead of foolhardy and arrogant.

"If anyone can do it you can, your highness," said Tatyana in her aging whore's voice. It would no longer go as sweetly high as she wanted to and crackled instead. Her brown hair was in its usual dishevelled mess. Tristan had watched it become more and more streaked with grey over the years. He preferred his whores older and experienced. He had no use for a maiden. But gold, adoration, and a hero's reputation, well, he had plenty of uses for those.

"But if your highness is just looking to play rescue," Tatyana continued, "I have two damsels in distress right here in dire need of liberation!" She shook her busty chest in his face, her breast almost spilling out the top of her corset.

Tristan pushed her away and she fell flat on her plump arse. The table howled with drunken laughter.

"The whore is right your majesty," said Braxis, the black market merchant. He was a hooded peddler of illegal goods and substances trading in everything from swords to sorcery.

He had also served on the Court of Repugnance the longest and was Tristan's most trusted adviser. "Your majesty is young, strong and an expert swordsman," he said. "The slaying of a lowly hag who probably has nothing more than cheap parlour tricks up her greasy sleeves should be easy work for you."

"And tell me, Braxis," asked Tristan, "where do you suppose I begin to look for this alleged tower? What if I end up chasing nothing but smoke and lies?"

"The tower is real your majesty," he whispered from under his hood, only his hooked nose poked out from the shadow. "I may even be able to provide you with a map to its location – provided I had the right resources. Treasure maps are, after all, so hard to come by these days."

Tristan rolled his eyes. In The Court of Repugnance no one ever did anything for free, least of all Braxis. But for the right price he could get hold of absolutely anything. He would have the crown plucked right off the king's head for the right amount of gold. "How much and when can you deliver the map to me?"

"For three hundred gold pieces and one of your fingernail clippings," said Braxis pretending to think. "I can have the map to you before dawn."

"A fingernail clipping?" Tristan asked, pulling his face into a pinched expression.

"The discarded matter of royalty holds great importance to some," said the merchant. "Witches use them to make their spells more efficacious."

Tristan thought for a moment before finally deciding. "Fine," he said, loosening his coin pouch from his belt and slipping it to Braxis. Tristan then gnawed off his longest fingernail and handed it to the merchant. "Meet me back here an hour before dawn and no later."

"I shall make it so, your majesty," Braxis bowed and floated backwards beyond the reach of the candle light into the darkness.

"Then it is decided," Tristan announced, slamming his wine goblet onto the table and standing up. "Tomorrow at dawn I shall ride to seek out this tower and all the wonders it's said to hold!"

The table exploded in a roar of applause and cheers.

"We shall tell all of your majesty's noble quest!" yelled Ortho.

"To victory!" said Sredence the Shadow raising his goblet.

"To victory indeed," said Tristan, raising his goblet in return.

Ω

TRUE TO HIS WORD, Braxis was there to meet Tristan in the Chamber of the Wretched an hour before dawn.

"I have secured the map as promised, your majesty," he said kneeling and holding up a wooden cylinder.

Tristan took the cylinder, opened the cap and slid out a thick parchment scroll. He scanned over the map that had been painted onto it. It was old and weathered but still readable.

"This journey will take at least three days," said Tristan gazing over the scale and key already calculating the best route to the tower.

"The road is long and treacherous," said Braxis. "I have

brought your majesty a few items you may find useful on this quest." He laid a leather bag at Tristan's feet.

"And what part of my body will all this cost me?"

"Two hundred gold pieces is a small price to ensure safe travel," said Braxis. His whisper echoed through the chamber like a small waterfall.

"Show me," said Tristan.

Braxis opened the bag and pulled out a leather necklace with a silver charm attached to it. He held the necklace up and the charm glittered in the candle light. "A protection amulet, your majesty. As long as you wear it, no enchantment can be placed upon you." He reached into the bag a second time and pulled out a vial of glowing blue liquid. "A magic potion, your majesty. Coat your sword with this and the blade will cut through any object, no matter how hard." He placed the necklace and vial next to each other on the floor before reaching back into the bag. This time he pulled out an ampule filled with a thick liquid the colour of chamber pot water. "This is a magical anti-venom. It can counteract the toxins from even the most deadly of fangs."

Tristan mulled the objects over. If he was going to accomplish this mission he wanted to do it on his own merits without the help of magical bric-à-brac that was likely useless anyway.

"I have no need for your expensive trinkets," said Tristan. "I have the map and that is all I require."

"Your majesty," Baxis protested, "this journey is a dangerous one. As skilled as you are, it would be ill-advised to take it without any kind of protection or assistance. Especially considering that you will be facing a witch."

"Spare me your pretence, Braxis," said Tristan raising his

hand. "You have made enough coin out of me for now. I will strike the crone down with a thousand blows if I have to, but the blows shall come from within me. Magic is for weaklings who cannot defend themselves with their own strength. You said yourself, all she may have are cheap parlour tricks."

"Very well, your majesty," said Braxis packing the items away. "If I may be so bold as to ask, what does your majesty intend to do with the maiden once he has rescued her?"

Tristan could not see the merchant's eyes but the undertone of lust in the man's voice came through loud and clear. "I haven't given the subject much thought," he said, rolling up the map. "At best, she could make the prettiest scullery made the palace has ever seen. At worst, who knows? I may be the one selling something to you for a change."

Ω

From the palace stables Tristan could see dawn breaking as a fine line of soft light on the horizon. He had made all the preparations and packed supplies the night before. Astrid, his blue roan neighed a greeting as she saw him walk through the stable doors.

"There's my girl!" said Tristan, running his hands through her mane. "Are you ready for an adventure?"

"Her and me both!" said a familiar voice from behind him. Tristan's heart sank as he turned around to see Alexander standing behind him.

"Alex. How did you find out I was going anywhere?"

"Your secret club isn't as secret as you think," Alex said. "You aren't the only one in the palace who knows about the hidden passages."

"You eavesdropped on the meeting with my court?! You're such a little snot! Go back to the palace. Quests are for princes, not princes and their child-bastard brothers."

"I'm not a child! I turn 14 in two months and I'm coming with you to rescue the fair maiden."

"Like hell you are," said Tristan, leading his horse passed Alex towards the stable doors.

"Take me with you," said Alex crossing his arms, "or I shall tell Father that man you brought inside the palace touched me."

Tristan stopped dead in his tracks at the threat. Dawn was breaking quickly and soon he would lose the cover of twilight and attract unwanted attention. He didn't have time to argue with his upstart of a little bastard half-brother. Tristan knew Alex would make good on his threat which could lead to massive problems for the Court of Repugnance. Their father would have every member of Tristan's network of outcasts hunted down if there was even a whisper of them bringing shame on the king's house. Alex may have been a bastard but he was the king's bastard and that came with certain perks.

"Don't slow me down," Tristan said, mounting Astrid and bolting out the stable.

Alex followed at an impressive pace on a sorrel mare called Lilly. The two darted out of the palace grounds and into the cobblestone streets of the city where the sleepy storefronts, taverns and brothels passed in a grey blur. Once outside the city walls, they joined the main road that split the surrounding forest and slowed the pace of their steeds to a steady canter.

"I had forgotten what a good rider you are," said Tristan.

"I used to have a good teacher," Alex replied.

Tristan recalled that a long time ago he had been the one to teach Alex how to ride. Tristan turned to gaze at his half-brother. He was not much to look at. Patches of the skin on his round face were inflamed with acne, his body soft and plump. He was an awkward child, not yet fully grown into his proportions.

"This is so exciting!" said Alex coming up to ride at Tristan's side, his chubby cheeks bouncing with the canter of the horse. "My first adventure!"

"I don't know what you are trying to prove tagging along with me like this," said Tristan as they made their way down the road. It had rained during the night and the ground was still sloppy. "And this isn't your adventure, it's mine."

"I have as much right to prove myself to Father as you do," said Alex. "And I'm going to do it by helping you."

"You don't understand a damn thing," laughed Tristan. "If you did, then you would know that I am not doing this to prove myself to Father. You could do ten quests just like this and he still wouldn't see you as anything more than a bastard and an obligation. I'm his legitimate son, heir to his throne and I can't even get him to respect me, what chance does a little castoff like you stand? Also, I don't need your help, I can do this on my own."

Tristan watched the bright optimism drain from his half-brother's cherub face. Alex slowed the pace of his horse to fall behind, becoming silent for the next few hours. Tristan didn't need to look back to see if Alex was still following him. The soggy pops of the second horse's hooves on the muddy road were never far behind.

They rode as the sun passed overhead until it began a

steady dip towards the horizon. Tristan pulled off the road and into the forest, riding until he was deep enough in to be sure he would be safe from highwaymen or drifters. He dismounted and stretched his legs. Alex, still behind him did the same without a word.

"You've packed for a small army," said Tristan looking at the saddle bags hanging from Lilly's sides. "The journey is only a few days."

"I wanted to be prepared in case we needed something," Alex responded not looking up from the bag he was unpacking.

Tristan caught a glimpse of something sticking out from one of the saddle bags. He walked over, reached into the bag and fished it out by its fluffy brown arm. Tristan knew the teddy bear, Sir Blackpaw. It was Alex's favourite childhood toy.

"Of course," said Tristan, holding it up. "God forbid we should need your filthy teddy bear and not have it."

"Give that to me!" Alex yelled as he saw Sir Blackpaw in Tristan's hand. He rushed over to grab it but Tristan held it up out of reach.

"Have you ever considered that people might treat you like less of a child if you stopped playing with toys?"

"It's not a toy!" Alex exclaimed, jumping up grabbing for the dangling bear. He missed it by just a centimetre. "I wouldn't expect you to understand. Now give it back to me!"

"What do you plan on doing with it?" Tristan laughed, holding the bear up a little higher. "Ask the witch if she wants to trade you? The maiden and treasure for a teddy bear?"

Bored with the game Tristan hurled the teddy bear into the woods and smirked at the sight of Alex running to retrieve it. "Just like a dog!" Tristan yelled after him. "I wonder what other useless garbage you hauled along with you!" He turned back to Alex's over-stuffed saddle bags, opened the flap and the smile dropped off his face like a weight.

"I'm allergic to them," said Alex, back from retrieving Sir Blackpaw. "But I know they're your favourite so I swiped some from the palace kitchen."

Tristan reached into the bag and pulled out one of the strawberries, perfectly ripe and red. He raised it to his lips and bit into it. Sweetness flooded the inside of his mouth. They really were his favourite. "Thanks," he said plainly before leaving to tend to Astrid.

After a small dinner of nuts and cured meats provided by Alex, the prince and his half-brother sat in silence. They stared into their campfire while darkness settled around them. The flames danced and cast shadows over their faces. Alex had not uttered a word since telling Tristan about the strawberries and the silence was making the prince uncomfortable. It was one thing to sit in silence when you were only in your own company, but it was another to be with someone and go so long without speaking.

"We used to sit by fires like this all the time," said Tristan, trying to stir up a conversation.

"I remember," said Alex. "Back when you were nice to me. We used to do a lot of things together. You taught me how to ride a horse and shoot an arrow. Now you only have time for whatever it is you get up to with your court of whatever. I've heard what the lords and ladies at court say about who you spend your time with. Father has also had a few choice words."

"I don't need a lecture on the company I keep," said Tristan, "least of all from a bastard child who has no idea what he's talking about."

"Then why don't you take some time out of your very busy princely schedule to explain it to me?" Alex asked, looking up from the fire. "Or does being a bastard make me too stupid to understand? Whoever did anything to you Your Majesty, to make you act the way you do? What is the reason a person handed everything in life, the very best of everything, is such a pompous prick?"

"You don't know the first thing about me," said Tristan. "Not everything is the way you think it is or want it to be and I don't have to explain myself to you."

"I thought that coming on this quest with you would be fun, that it would give us a chance to connect again. You say you can't stand Father but you are just like him. You look down on anyone who isn't you or does things differently to you. You even look at me the same way Father does, like I'm nothing but a mistake that isn't supposed to be here. Well I am here, Tristan, and I'm doing the best I can to show you both that I'm more than what you dismiss me for. I suppose dismissing people comes naturally to princes and kings."

"Stop being so desperate to please everyone," said Tristan. "It's pathetic. I don't want to be a king! I don't even want to be a prince!"

"Who wouldn't want to be a prince or a king?" Alex asked. "Would you prefer the life of a pathetic bastard? You could be a better king than Father, you could help people! That's what I would do if I were you."

"Well thank God you aren't me," said Tristan turning away from Alex to end the conversation.

"Here!" said Alex, throwing one of the cotton-stuffed pillows he had packed at Tristan, hitting him in the back. "Your fat head will need it if you want to get a good night's sleep."

Ω

Traveling with Alex turned out to be more advantageous than Tristan was willing to admit. Alex had packed supplies that made the journey a lot more bearable. Half way through the second day it started to rain and he pulled out two waterproof leather cloaks with hoods. He had even brought along a small supply of dried oats and molasses for the horses. He was good with the steeds. When they set up camp on the second night both horses chose to be near him.

"Astrid prefers you to me," said Tristan.

"That's because you have good common sense, don't you girl?" he said to the horse while petting her face. She nuzzled him with her snout and he fed her a handful of oats. "Do you expect to reach the tower before dark tomorrow?"

"I don't think so," said Tristan, pouring over the map. "But definitely before midday the following day."

"Seems pretty random to me," said Alex, stretching out. "A single tower in the middle nowhere."

"My guess is that it's all that's left of a long ruined castle or something like that," said Tristan.

"What do you plan on doing with all the treasure and the maiden?" asked Alex.

"Does it matter?" said Tristan. "The point was just to get it done."

"I don't believe that for a second."

"Believe whatever you like," Tristan grumbled.

"Why are you like this?" Alex asked, sitting up. "When did you stop caring about everything?"

"I care about things," said Tristan. "They just aren't the things everyone thinks I should care about."

"Enlighten me then," said Alex, crossing his arms.

"The point isn't to do it," said Tristan. "The point is to prove to myself and everyone else that I *could* do it. The treasure and the tart are just an added bonus. Though some riches of my own would be nice, then I wouldn't have Father breathing fire down my neck for spending his money on drink and whores. If I'm lucky, there will be enough treasure for me to leave Thraxia forever."

"You are Father's only heir," said Alex, confused. "You would leave the kingdom without a king?"

"We've been through this," said Tristan. "I told you I don't want to be king and I don't want to talk about it anymore. I am sure one of our airhead cousins would love to take my place."

Alex was silent for a moment, like he was considering something before he spoke. "I've never been with a whore," he said changing the subject. Tristan felt the heat from his half-brother's round blushing cheeks from the other side of the campsite. "I've never been with any girl."

"I suppose you just prefer men then," said Tristan. Alex went quiet again, choosing not to be baited into ridicule. Tristan let out a sigh. "You are still young," he said trying to be gentler. "There will be plenty of time for that kind of thing."

Alex shook his head. "I doubt it. And even if it was so, it wouldn't be the same as it is for you. Women fall for you like apples from trees on a windy autumn day. I wouldn't be surprised if at the end of the night the whores were the ones paying you."

"You talk such nonsense," said Tristan. "And it's *very* clear you have never been with a whore. They turn into gorgons if they are not paid, no matter who they've been with."

"It's not nonsense!" Alex protested. "You should hear how the woman at court talk about you!" He raised the back of his hand to his forehead and pretended to swoon. "Ooh Prince Tristan," he said in a voice three pitches above his natural tone. "Those muscles! Those eyes! Those lips! He drives me wild! Take me now, Prince Tristan!" He began to convulse on the ground in pelvic thrusts. "Oh Prince Tristan, you've ripped my garters!"

Tristan burst into thunderous laughter. "You do a good impression, albeit a highly exaggerated one."

Alex returned to his normal voice. "My point is women will never talk about me like that."

"It's not about how you look, though it doesn't hurt to be dashingly handsome. It's all in the way you carry yourself. I can teach you."

"I don't think that kind of thing can be learned," said Alex.

"It can! You can learn it as easily as you learned to ride a horse," said Tristan. "When we get back to the palace I'll show you."

Alex scoffed. "Please, when we get back to the palace you'll forget all about me again. It will be just as it was before, only worse because you will have all your treasure and glory to keep you occupied."

"No!" said Tristan. "I swear it! When we get back to the palace I'll show you how to get girls to like you."

"I'll believe it when I see it," said Alex.

"Oh you will," said Tristan. "I promise."

Ω

"Do you smell them?" Saskia asked, her nostrils flaring. She stuck her tongue out to taste the air.

"I do indeed," said Vagabond, drool gushing from her lips. "A prince! He reeks of royalty! So sweet and tender! And another, a young companion, plump and juicy!"

"I prefer the taste of blacksmith," Mabmoria hissed through her jagged teeth. "Toughened by toil and ripened by flame."

"But prince is what we have today. Maybe next time it will be blacksmith," Saskia replied.

"Baker is best," said Vagabond. "They taste of treats."

Saskia continued to lick the air greedily. "He rides upon a blue roan and his heartbeat is strong with excitement. His squire rides beside him."

"We haven't had horse in centuries," said Vagabond as she continued to drool. "Could we eat the horse too?"

"Don't be stupid! Horses can't climb towers," scolded Mabmoria.

The stomach they shared began to lurch and growl. "So hungry," moaned Vagabond.

"Hungry indeed," moaned Mabmoria.

"Patience, sisters. He will soon be ours! Both of them if we are lucky and clever!" Saskia said. "Shall we lower the lure?"

"Ooh! The hair of the maiden fair!" Mabmoria cackled.

"So that he may rescue her and claim the fabled treasures of the tower!"

"He is *supposed* to ask first! That is how we are *supposed* to do it!" Vagabond spat back.

"We can do it however we like!" said Saskia. "It is our lie to bend as we please! I'm bored with them asking! Let's get him up here as soon as possible so we may feast!"

"Lower the lure," said Mabmoria. "I want to taste his excitement!"

"Shall I sing for him?" asked Vagabond.

"Yes!" Saskia and Mabmoria hissed in unison. "Sing for him sister! Entice him! Call to him!"

Saskia peered into the field through the asphodel below the tower. "I see them! The prince is muscular and handsome and his squire is plump! So much flesh!"

"I cannot wait to suck the marrow from their bones!" said Vagabond, rubbing their hands together.

"It is good to eat so regularly for so little work," said Mabmoria. "We are as skilled at weaving lies as we are at weaving web!"

"So clever of us!" Saskia agreed. "So clever and so treacherous!"

Ω

"I can't believe we're here!" Alex said, coming up behind Tristan.

Tristan shot him a dirty look as he put his index finger to his lips. "Be quiet," he whispered. "We don't really know what we are walking into."

"Oh, right," said Alex in a much quieter voice.

The tower loomed in front of them. It was truly a sight to behold. The grey stone structure stood tall, planted firmly in the centre of a meadow of asphodel in full bloom. The spring sun shone down with a warm light.

Tristan's eyes ran up the length of the lonely structure. At the top stood a single window, just as the legend said.

"Looks like you won't need to ask the maiden to let down her hair," said Alex. "It would seem she has already done so."

Alex was right. Long golden hair braided together as thick as shipping rope bellowed out of the open window. It danced in the sweet summer breeze, perfumed by the scent of wild flowers, river water and sunlight. The hair glittered, beckoning Tristan to come closer, to touch it, to climb it.

"Maybe she heard we were coming," said Tristan, unable to take his eyes off the golden trusses. The air carried a tune being sung from inside the tower. It echoed through his mind:

True and brave, from far and near, I call to you, lend me your ear.

Rescuer bold, rescuer strong, I've waited now my whole life long.

Climb up to me, and you will see, that you and I are meant to be.

Rescuer brave, rescuer true, here by my loom, I wait for you.

"Do you hear that?" Tristan asked.

Alex looked around. "Hear what? I don't hear anything."

"She's singing," said Tristan. "She's singing for me."

"Tristan, I don't know about this," Alex said, sceptical. "Something doesn't feel right about this place. I feel like we're being watched. It's the witch, she is eyeing us!"

"Don't be such a coward," Tristan said, his eyes still fixed to the tower. He dug his heels into Astrid's sides to urge her forward but the mare would go no further.

"Even the horses are spooked," said Alex, trying to get control over Lilly who kept backing away from the tower. "I think we should go."

"If you want to stay here and play with your teddy bear, that's fine," said Tristan. "But I'm going to get what I came here for." He dismounted his horse. With his sword sheathed on his back he made the rest of the way to the base of the tower on foot. Alex grew smaller and smaller behind him as he walked.

He had not travelled this far to turn back now. Riches beyond imagination, the adoration of the maiden and freedom, out from under his father's thumb were well within his reach. A chill came over him as he approached. The asphodel blossoms turned on their stems to look at him as he passed. The small white flowers let out a collection of soft sighs. Undeterred, Tristan continued, the maiden's sweet song calling out to him. Soon she and the treasure held captive with her would be his.

He reached out his hand and gathered the glittering locks in his palm. Her hair was soft as rose petals and twice as fragrant. Tristan's senses were overwhelmed with her song in his ears, her hair in his hand and her smell in his nose. They were all working together, making him want her more than he had ever wanted anything. He was drunk on her, whoever she was. His grip on her hair tightened and he hoisted himself up, placing the souls of his feet against the tower wall. Across the field Astrid, Lilly and Alex looked on. The horses kicked and neighed, tugging hard at the reigns.

"Be careful!" yelled Alex.

But Tristan didn't hear him. The maiden's song was the only thing his ears wanted to know. He made quick work of the climb, taking care not to look down, especially when he reached the top. He got a firm grip on the ledge of the window and pulled himself up.

From the ground Alex watched as something long and pale reached out of the dark window, grabbed his half-brother and pulled him in.

Ω

TRISTAN WAS JERKED SHARPLY through the open window and fell to a wet and sticky floor. His left hand was caught on something. He couldn't pull free. His eyes adjusted to his new surroundings, just enough light broke through the window for him to make out what was going on. As far as he could see the room had been draped in dense white webs. The hair he had climbed up on was just more webbing that on the inside of the tower went up towards the rafters and merged into more web. Directly ahead of him was the entrance to a tunnel big enough to ride a horse through, also made up of the pearly white strands as thick as wool. The entrance of the web tunnel let out a heavy draught that brought with it the foul smell of rot and damp.

His left arm was stuck to a thick wad of fresh web that dripped with a sticky substance. Tristan unsheathed his sword from his back with his free hand and swiped at the web but the blade did not cut through. Instead it too became stuck and the prince could not pull it free.

A sharp cackle echoed through the opening of the tunnel.

"Who goes there?" Tristan demanded to know only to be met with more cackling.

"Hello, sweet prince," whispered a course voice through the thick forest of web. "We've been waiting for you." More vicious laughter broke out and reverberated through the tower.

Tendrils of web shot towards Tristan from the opening of the tunnel and wrapped around him, enclosing his body in a cocoon. Something on the other end of the tunnel began pulling him towards the dark entrance and whatever horrors awaited him inside. He struggled against the pull of the web but lost his footing and fell to the floor, smacking his head so hard a flash burst over his vision. The sticky white vines pulled him closer until he was swallowed by the dark mouth of the tunnel.

He slid down the tunnel and landed with a soft bounce in the centre of an intricately weaved net. A sharp jab broke through his cocoon and landed in his side. After the initial sting came a searing throb. He screamed.

"Hush now," said a voice from the gloom around him. "It will be over soon."

Tristan opened his eyes. The room was lit by low burning candles and in the centre, right in front of him, sat what could only be the witch.

A withered grey corpse of a body with a distended belly and sagging wrinkled breasts lounged on a throne of bones. The top of the torso split into three different necks, each crowned by a hideous head. This was no witch. This was a monstrous abomination. A creature that had died centuries ago but somehow still clung to life. From the top of each head sprouted long sharp horns and behind them grew thick strands of grey hair that stretched to merge with the web around them. Tristan was having trouble breathing thanks to whatever venom he had been poisoned with. The searing pain was spreading from his side across the rest of his body.

"Unhand me. Tell me where the maiden is and I may spare your miserable life!" Tristan said.

The three ghoulish heads cackled, black tears oozing from the hollow sockets where their eyes should have been.

"You are looking at her!" shrieked the middle head, still fitting with laughter.

"Fair maiden indeed!" squawked the left head. "Are my sisters and I not the most fair of maidens you have ever laid eyes upon?"

The monster continued to shriek with laughter, gripping its rotting sides in vicious hilarity.

A pit formed in Tristan's stomach. It had all been an elaborate trap. His heart slammed in his chest, pushing the burning venom through his body, numbing his senses and clouding his mind. In his line of site there hung at least 30 corpses tangled in the webs of hair. Some wore armour, some just tunics but all had been drained of life, fluids and flesh by the creature of the tower.

"Do you like our treasures?" asked the right head. "I hope you do. We've spent so long putting together our little collection."

At that moment, Tristan heard a rattle come from the end of the tunnel behind him, followed quickly by the echoes of something that was more than a scream but less than a war cry. Alex came flying through the opening of the tunnel, screaming the best war cry he could muster. He brandished his own sword that cut right through the net of a web. He landed on his feet in front of the monster.

"Get away from my brother," he said holding his sword ready to strike.

The damage done to the net left Tristan dangling in his cocoon at a strange angle. The tethers holding him in place snapped and he fell to the cold stone floor.

"So glad you could join us, little one," hissed the middle head. "We've been dying for a two course meal!"

The creature rose up from its throne. From its back two long limbs grew, at the end of which sat sharp stingers dripping with milky venom.

"Alex, be careful!" Tristan shouted.

Alex didn't take his eyes off the monster as it lashed out and swiped at him. He managed to dodge each attack while getting in a few good swipes of his own. As hazy as Tristan was he understood what Alex was doing. He wasn't strong enough to overpower the monster so he was going to tire it out instead, before delivering a killing blow.

The monster sent its right stinger hurtling down toward Alex but he dodged it just in time. The stinger hit the floor instead. Alex spun around and severed the stinger off in one sweep of his sword. The monster screeched in agony as tar-like blood poured from the end of its now amputated limb. Alex saw his chance and took it. He jumped forward and in another single swipe lopped off all three of the monster's hideous heads.

The moment his sword hit the monster's necks, the monster lashed out with its remaining stinger, lodging it in Alex's back. The last bit of life shook itself free of the monster, its body went limp and the stinger fell away from the wound it inflicted. Alex fell to his knees and his sword clattered to the floor.

Tristan couldn't move, he was still trapped inside the cocoon. The venom was working quickly. He had lost sensation in half his body and the numbness was spreading. "Alex!" Tristan called out as loudly as his poisoned voice would allow.

Alex crawled over to Tristan, dragging his sword behind him. He fumbled to get a good grip on the hilt but managed to cut Tristan free of his webbed cage. Alex leaned forward and something silver fell from the inside of his shirt. It was the protection amulet Braxis had tried to sell Tristan.

"Alex, where did you-"

"There isn't time," said Alex. The veins in his neck and face were swelling and his bloodshot eyes were bulging away from their sockets. He coughed and blood splattered from his mouth. With shaking hands, Alex reached for the leather satchel tied to his side, spilling its contents on the floor. The satchel held an empty vial that once contained the potion for the sword, and Sir Blackpaw. He used his sword to cut into the back of the teddy bear revealing the ampule of anti-venom.

Alex snapped the top of the ampule open and lowered it to Tristan's mouth. Tristan grabbed Alex's arm to stop him.

"There's only enough for one of us," said Tristan.

"I know," said Alex. "It has to be you. Thraxia can't be left without an heir to the throne. You have to live. You have to rule."

"I can't let you do this," said Tristan.

Alex freed his arm from Tristan's grip and poured the anti-venom passed the prince's lips. The foul liquid filled

Tristan's mouth and he swallowed hard. "I'm so sorry," he said through the tears that were falling from his eyes.

Alex fell on his back and closed his eyes. His breathing had become shallow and swollen veins ran black over his body. Tristan crawled to his brother's side. "Alex, you need to hold on, I can get us out of here. We can find more medicine. I can go get help."

Alex grabbed Tristan's hand and pulled him closer. "No, don't leave me," he wheezed against the blood flooding his lungs. Colour was abandoning his body. Blood was pooling underneath him from the wound in his back.

"Alex, please hold on," wailed Tristan, resting his sobbing face against his brother's chest. "I'm so sorry."

"Ssh," Alex hushed. "Thank you for the adventure."

"Don't go Alex!" Tristan cried. "I have to keep my promise, remember?" Tristan gently touched Alex's face in an attempt to keep him conscious, it was clammy with sweat and sticky with blood. "I have to teach you how to get girls to like you. Don't you want to learn?"

Alex didn't respond. His shallow breaths had stopped and his hold on Tristan's hand fell loose. Tristan threw his face in his hands and screamed.

The anti-venom had worked but Tristan wished it hadn't. He looked over through his tear-blurred eyes at the teddy bear with the stuffing pulled from its back. He picked the bear up and tried to push the stuffing back inside, but the cut was too wide. Alex's mother had made it for him before she died. Tristan knew this and had still chosen to tease Alex with it. Alex was right, Tristan was just as much of a monster as their father. He remembered when Alex was little and couldn't go to sleep at night without Sir Blackpaw by his side. The inside of Tristan's chest shattered like a mirror at the thought and he choked on his tears. He placed the bear on Alex's chest and folded the dead boy's hands over his childhood companion.

A day ago he had told Alex, he didn't owe him an explanation for his behaviour, for abandoning him when he became more interested with carving his own path to glory than catching frogs in rivers or taking horseback rides through the kingdom. Now all Tristan wanted to do was explain and apologise, but it was too late. Dead ears don't hear.

He looked around the dark room, there was plenty of web he could use to hang himself. That was what he wanted to do but it would mean his fallen brother's sacrifice would be for nothing. He couldn't let that happen, he needed to go on, if not for himself then for Alex.

He looked around the gloomy pit, the candles burning low, their light fading. He didn't want to leave Alex in that awful place, alone in the dark, but he wasn't strong enough to pull them both back through the tunnel.

"I'll come back for you, I promise," said Tristan believing that no matter what, this time he would keep his word. He thought of his brother's kindness and wit. "You were more of a prince than I ever was and more of a king than I ever hope to be."

Ω

THE DAMAGE DONE by the monster's venom never fully healed. Tristan carried it with him for the rest of his days, along with the guilt of his brother's death. But he had made good on his promise. When he was well enough he returned to the tower to retrieve Alex's remains and have the tower destroyed. He couldn't do anything to fix the ruined past but there was still time to fix the future. Tristan dissolved the Court of Repugnance, wanting nothing more to do with whores, murderers and chasing after shallow glory. Instead he turned his attention towards helping making the kingdom of Thraxia better for her citizens. When the king died Tristan took to the throne fully prepared to lead as the most magnanimous ruler the kingdom would ever see.

At night when King Tristan went to bed, he sometimes dreamed of Alex. They would go on long rides through the kingdom, talk by the river, catch frogs and laugh together. In the king's dreams everything was as it should have been.

15
MYTHICA

"I'm alone now," she said. "The rest of the gods faded into nothing after people stopped believing in them. But not me. I will not allow that to happen to me. I will never be forgotten." Mythica sat at the end of her dressing room in her make-up chair, looking at her reflection in the mirror as she spoke.

Her dressing room was everything Alex expected. Clean and crisp, floor to ceiling. It was brightly lit with white candles and white roses everywhere – the drag queen's favourite flower. That was one of the questions on the questionnaire Alex had answered in order to win the ticket to meet Mythica, the Legendary Drag Queen. A once in a life time, one-on-one meet and greet opportunity, or so the marketing material on the website had read.

Alex's mother had warned that one should never meet their heroes. At the time Alex had just shrugged it off as the bitter cynicism, but now he was starting to wander if mother did indeed know best.

"Long ago," Mythica continued, "beyond the reaches of

human memory and record, before anything else, there was only he and I. He created everything from the waters of primordial chaos and the tasked me to fly around the universe in my chariot and set fire to every star in the universe." She sounded like the narrator of a bad movie.

Alex blinked slowly and didn't know where to look. *She is as crazy as everyone says she is.*

"That was a very impolite thought," Mythica said.

"How did you know what I was thinking?" Alex asked, stunned. Was it a lucky guess, he wondered?

Mythica rolled her eyes and her gold eyeshadow glittered. "I told you, I'm a goddess."

"A goddess?" Alex questioned further, cringing a little. "As in Hera and Zeus and Aphrodite?"

Mythica continued to look at herself in her mirror as she primped her hair. It was the colour of champagne, cascading down her back in loose waves. "Child, I am the one their myths are based on. I'm the OG: Original Goddess. Zeus got his wrath from me, Hera her pettiness and Aphrodite…well," she paused, admiring herself further in the mirror. "I think it's pretty obvious what she got from me. You know, my husband once asked me if I would ever get tired of looking at my own reflection. It's been literally *millennia* and the answer is still no."

"Anyway, I think I need to be going now," said Alex, getting up from the white sofa. This meeting was not what he had expected. He knew that Mythica wasn't like other drag queens – that is what he liked about her – but he was hoping underneath the grand façade and spectacular performances he would get to meet a person that he could connect with. This wasn't it.

Mystery had surrounded Mythica since she burst onto the drag scene five years ago. No one knew where she came from, or anything else about her. The world was full of drag queens whose male alter egos were just as well-known as their drag personas but Mythica was just Mythica. She was never seen or photographed out of drag, which led many to believe that she wasn't actually male at all. That didn't matter to Alex, he didn't care how his idol identified or what was between their legs, he only cared about the art.

The internet was flooded with conspiracy theories and rumours but nothing had ever been confirmed. The mystery of Mythica is what made her interesting, but her performances and music are what drew people to her in droves. She used state of the art technology to put on light shows that left audiences in awe – and some in the throes of photosensitive epileptic fits. Her shows came with warnings but for those who could safely attend it was a mind altering experience. Some theorised that she made use of drones and lasers to project images that would transfer her audiences into the heart of far-off nebulas, star glittered asteroid fields and dying suns. Others spoke of augmented reality technology. Whatever it was, Alex had seen Mythica perform several times and each time was a new experience. Her concerts were filled with light, colour, hypnotic dancing and music like the siren songs of legend. Her shows weren't something that could be captured by a video camera or explained. You had to *be* there, you had to *live* it. Her performances were also something that no one had yet been able to replicate. Only Mythica could do what she did. This left drag fans and scientists alike totally confounded and equally impressed.

"Figures," Mythica said, sounding indifferent, not taking

her eyes off the mirror, "I finally want to tell someone the truth and they don't want to listen. Some Little Supernova you turned out to be. Super disappointment more like."

Little Supernovas was the name Mythica used for her fan base. It played well into her brand of light and space, but Alex wasn't going to be manipulated by a deluded prima-donna wannabe. "It was nice to meet you," he said politely before lifting himself off the sofa and heading for the door.

The lightbulbs around the mirror suddenly burned brighter as Alex reached for the door handle. The candle flames grew taller and the dressing room began to feel more like a sauna.

"No," Mythica commanded, turning in her chair to face Alex directly for the first time since he entered the dressing room. "You will hear what I have to say."

An invisible force punched Alex in the stomach and sent him straight back onto the sofa. Alex watched as the vase of white roses next to the sofa was toppled. Before it hit the floor it froze mid-air and performed a live-action rewind. The vase and flowers returned perfectly to their place, as they were in the moment before they were knocked over. Alex started looking around for hidden cameras.

"Am I on some kind of prank show?" Alex asked. "You can come out now! I know what is going on!"

Mythica shot him a bored stare and sighed. "If you don't believe me then I will just have to show you." The drag queen's eyes widened and Alex's locked onto them. Alex couldn't look away and was pulled further and further into the hot white light of her gaze until everything around them was obliterated in a bright flash.

Alex was floating weightless in a black abyss. He fumbled

around in the cold dark chasm, floundering for something to grab on to so he could steady himself. Everything was black. Had he died? Is this what being dead was like?

"In the beginning, there really was nothing," Mythica's hypnotic warm voice echoed around the abyss, coming from everywhere and nowhere at the same time. "Until a spark of light ignited and from it burst the primordial waters of chaos and us with it."

As she spoke, so it was. A spark did indeed ignite. A fraction of a second later Alex was thrown away from it in an explosion of glittering matter that he somehow knew would soon make up everything in the universe.

"It was then we came into existence," said Mythica's disembodied voice. "Divine beings of warmth, life and light."

The glittering primordial waters swirled and flowed in the empty space like clouds. The clouds parted, making way for an emerging light that grew brighter and brighter until everything was enveloped in its heat.

"We formed the chaos into order, creating the galaxies, stars and planets with our force of will," Mythica said, appearing for the first time in her human form, but at the same time so much more. She stood tall and proud upon a golden chariot drawn by a great comet. Alex gazed at her and knew that she was the true source of all light in the universe. Every inch of the goddess shone with an ethereal glow. She charged across the universe leaving a trail of bursting new stars in her wake.

"Life exploded across creation. One planet in particular caught our attention. It was different from all the others, unique in its beauty and the life that thrived upon it. It was the planet that would one day be known as Earth."

Alex floated towards a familiar site: Earth. Shining and filled with new life. He was then brought closer to see humans that lived ages before him constructing great temples adorned with precious metals and stones. Inside one of the temples upon a towering throne sat Mythica in all her glory. Thousands of worshipers crowded at her feet, leaving offerings and adoration.

"Here the inhabitants of the planet would come to worship us as the gods we were, and in return for their worship, we nourished them. We had not brought them life directly, but we did teach them how to live. We showed them how to erect temples and monuments in our honour. I taught them how to navigate using my children, the stars of the sky, to guide their way. We made them strong, that was our first and greatest mistake."

Alex did not recognise the ancient civilizations that rose before his eyes. Their buildings, farm lands, cities expanded far and wide. He witnessed all of it, their lives, their deaths, their marvellous victories and disastrous losses.

"Greed comes so easily to humans. No matter how much we gave them they still hungered for more. As they grew stronger they began to war with one another, tearing asunder all we had tried to teach them. Over time they began to distance themselves from us, finding new and different versions of us to worship. False gods they created to suit their own narratives and beliefs. Thousands of gods rose and fell from the mire of collective human consciousness, each one more bastardized than the last until they had grown so far from us that they no longer knew who we truly were."

Alex continued to watch the ancient tale Mythica was narrating unfold before his eye.

"But it was too late for us," she said. "We had grown too reliant on human worship for our own existence which in turn had become a shadow of what it once was. We were addicted to the worship and would accept it in whatever diluted form we could find. We began to play into whatever narrative the humans would come up with, just to sustain ourselves. My husband would appear to them in whichever form was trending at the time – a swan, an eagle, and a burning bush were just a few of the masks he wore. I would do the same, appearing as angels and virgin mothers. If they were looking for a sign we would give it to them. My husband and I began to grow apart until we no longer recognised each other. We were forced to take separate paths so that we could maintain the dry husk of what our existence had become."

A pearly tear fell from the goddess's eye and rolled down her cheek. In that tear Alex could see the longing she held inside herself for a life she no longer lived.

"Time passed and we faded into the shadows," she continued, "our images twisted and changed by humanity until they no longer resembled any part of what we were. After more time even the bastardizations were forgotten. I fell into a space beyond myth but I refused to fade away. The constantly unwinding path of time has brought me to where I am now. Mythica Goddess of Light! Worship me!"

Alex recognised those last words. They were the ones used at the opening of every one of Mythica's performances. He was pulled to the front row of a Mythica concert. Her fans screamed and clapped for her while she danced, sang and performed her light show, which Alex now knew had nothing to do with projector-mounted drones or laser beams. It was all her. Every explosion of light and colour, every nebula and star came directly from the tips of her fingers and the breath of her lungs. She was drawing power in from the applause and giving it back through performance. The concert began to fade away until the adoring fans and stage vanished. Alex was back in the dressing room, seated on the white leather couch next to the goddess who was older than time itself.

He sat still and drew in the sweet scent of white roses and melting candle wax. His head was spinning, being back inside of his body felt constrained after flying through the fabric of space and time. He slowly came back into himself until he felt grounded enough to speak.

"So you are a goddess, pretending to be a man that pretends to be a woman?" Alex asked.

"No," Mythica said plainly. "I am a primordial being that was deified as a goddess who is now pretending to be a human male that pretends to be a woman *for money.*"

"What?" Alex asked, screwing up his face as he tried to understand what Mythica had just said.

"You're very labelled obsessed, kid," she said. "Not a good look during this whole non-binary movement. Very problematic."

"I just don't understand," said Alex. "You could be anything or anyone. You could be the biggest pop star the world has ever seen. Why did you choose to become just low-key famous amongst a minority group?"

"I only take what I need," she said. "If humanity has taught me one thing, it's that greed is dangerous. I saw what was going on in the drag scene and I wanted to be a part of it. The community appeals to me. You say gender is on a spectrum.

Well, so is light. Even stars are binary and non-binary. How could a goddess of light and life resist?"

"Why are you telling me all of this?" Alex asked.

"Even goddesses get lonely," she said, looking away from him. "I wanted to know what it would be like to share what I really am with someone. Even if it was just one person. Do you regret me telling you? Showing you?"

Alex was still for a moment before responding. "I don't know. It's changed the way I see everything. I came here hoping to connect with you. When you first started speaking, I didn't think that was going to happen and now it turns out I got a lot more than I bargained for."

"Go well, my Little Supernova," she said. "Thank you for letting me tell you my story. And please, whatever you do, don't start a cult in my name. I hate it when that happens. The worship I get is great but it *never* ends well for the people in the cult."

Alex laughed but then his mind wandered toward a more serious topic. "Aren't you afraid I'm going to tell everyone?"

Mythica got up from the sofa, sat back down in front of her mirror and started preening herself again. "Bitch please," she said, flipping her hair back. "As if anyone would believe you."

"Thank you," he said, standing up and walking towards the door. "It was good to get to know you. The real you." She turned in her chair to look at Alex for the last time. She said nothing, just nodded her head and smiled.

Alex closed the dressing room door behind him and was escorted out of the venue. It still felt strange being back inside his body, like he hadn't fully come down to Earth yet and maybe never would. He floated out of the venue through a mist of his own thoughts. At the exit, he was handed a hamper stuffed with Mythica merchandise. Images of the goddess stared back at him from t-shirts and mugs with some of her most popular catch phrases.

Radiate with me, read one of the t-shirts.

Dance at the speed of light, was printed on a phone case.

Rise and refract, commanded a coffee mug with the image of Mythica inside a star.

As Alex walked towards his car. In the quiet night he looked up at the stars with new eyes. He loved drag. It made him appreciate that everything is so much more than it seemed. As he started the engine and drove off, he felt that appreciation ran deeper now than it ever had before. Maybe his mother had turned out to be wrong and you should meet your heroes after all.

16
FIRST DAY JITTERS

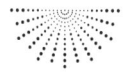

"Welcome to your induction. I'm the demon Naberius and I'll be your facilitator."

The deep voice sounded bored as it echoed through Chris's ears. His head was spinning and he was still trying to make sense of things. His cloudy vision began to clear and he took in his surroundings. The voice, he realised, had come from the terrifying creature that stood in front of him. The red, scaly demon towered over Chris, it was at least eight feet tall. It leered at him with bright yellow eyes through rimless oval glasses. It held a black clipboard in one claw and a pen in the other.

Chris rubbed his eyes. "Are you wearing a business suit?" he asked.

"My clown suit is at the dry cleaners, sorry about that," said the demon rolling his eyes and exposing a mouthful of milky fangs.

The two of them stood in a dark hallway of polished obsidian. The walls were decorated with frescos of people screaming and being tortured by winged beasts. The support pillars were made from melted black glass and jagged spikes protruded from them in random places. Behind the demon's leathery bat wings, Chris could see the entrance to the hallway lit by bright fire.

"Wait, am I in Hell?" Chris asked.

"Not at all," said the demon. "You're at the frozen yoghurt shop at the mall. Open your eyes! Look around you, cupcake. Take in all the fire and brimstone!"

"But if I'm in Hell," it suddenly dawned on Chris, "then that means I'm dead."

The demon looked over the top of his glasses and raised one eyebrow. "You must have been a real rocket scientist back on Earth."

"How did I die? I don't remember dying," said Chris, patting his torso. He was still solid and still in one piece.

"Look, Rocket Scientist. I don't have all day," the demon huffed. "So excuse me if I skip all the existential dread you're feeling right now. Trust me, it'll pass. Hell isn't as bad as everyone makes it out to be." A bone chilling scream rattled through the hallway. "Well, at least not so bad for *everyone*. Grab one of the pitchforks off the wall and we'll get started."

"Started with what?" Chris asked as he lifted one of the pitchforks off a hook on the wall. It was light and made of the same glassy material as the pillars. Its prongs were long and serrated. The staff was perfect for jabbing and stabbing at a distance.

"Your tour, Rocket Scientist! Come on! We've all got work to do and the boss gets real pissy if we don't meet target."

"I'm so confused," said Chris as he followed the demon out of the hallway and into the bowels of Hell.

He tried to take it all in but there was so much going on it was impossible. As far as his eyes could see stretched a vast expanse of flaming plains and caverns filled with the suffering, the miserable and the damned. Hell looked how every god-fearing Christian believed it would, complete with a lake of fire. A boiling wind bellowed through the scream-filled air and rustled Chris's hair.

"I don't understand," he said. "What did I do to deserve being sent to Hell?"

"It's not about what you did or didn't do," said the demon. "When your time came, the powers that be decided your talents would be best put to use here."

"But I don't deserve to be punished," said Chris. "I was a good person...for the most part." Chris had always existed in that weird place of being raised to be religious when he was a kid, but where the religion had never quite stuck. He wasn't a saint but he didn't do any of the really bad things, nothing that would get him eternal damnation. At least that is what he thought. He was having trouble remembering what his life had been or even how he'd died. "Why can't I remember anything? My life and how I died – it's all gone."

"You aren't here to remember," said the demon. "That part of your soul's journey is over. You aren't here to be punished either, Rocket Scientist." The demon looked down at the pitchfork in Chris's hands. "You are here *to* punish."

"What?" Chris asked, confused.

"We're a little short staffed, okay?" said the demon. "HR decided it would be a good idea to outsource torturer positions. Give it a try. You might even like it." The demon motioned towards a flaming pit crammed with screaming people. They were on fire but weren't burning away.

"Who are those guys?" Chris asked.

"Police officers who took bribes," said the demon. "We've got a lot of politicians down here too. Stab 'em."

Chris rolled the pitchfork over in his palms. "I mean...I guess I could. If you say they were bad people then they had it coming."

"That's the spirit!" said the demon, looking enthusiastic. He pointed out a man at the far left of the pit. "That guy was a cop who tried to get a bribe out of you one time. When you wouldn't pay, he intimidated and arrested you."

The wheels in Chris's head turned and he remembered the cop. Two years before his death, Chris had spent a weekend in jail on wrongful charges because of that cop. When he was released, Chris's record was expunged but there were no consequences for the cop and his blatant abuse of power.

"Oh, *fuck* that guy," he said before jamming the pitchfork right into the tortured souls face, piercing his right eye. A tingle of pleasure resonated up his spine and his body shivered.

The demon smiled. "It's fun to punish people who screwed us over."

The tingling sensation fizzed over Chris's forehead before quickly vanishing. He lifted his hands to his face and felt that two small lumps had formed on either side of his forehead. "What's happening to me?" he asked, quickly running both hands over the lumps to give them a better feel.

"Those are just your horns coming in," said the demon, checking something off in the notes on his clipboard. "It's nothing to worry about. Just the first of several physical changes you'll go through over the next few days."

"What do you mean?" Chris asked, breaking out into a cold sweat.

"Well if you work in Hell you have to look the part," said the demon. "Think of it like a uniform."

"You mean I'm going to end up looking like you?" Chris asked. The smooth red scales that covered the demon's body glittered in the firelight of the pits. Chris looked up at the two dark long horns that protruded sharply from the demon's forehead. He remembered the forked tongue that had made more than one appearance over the course of their interaction. It would slither out from behind the demon's viper fangs. Chris looked into the demon's yellow snake eyes and shivered.

The demon laughed. "You should be so lucky! But yes, it's all part of the gig. So, like I said, we have a lot of politicians down here too. The particularly bad ones have their own special place, but don't worry, everyone gets a chance to have a go at them at least once a month, sometimes twice if the roster allows."

"Good to know," said Chris, still unsure.

The demon crossed his tree trunk arms. "My point is, don't make the mistake of thinking there isn't anyone here who doesn't really deserve to be here. Bribery and corruption were the least of that cop's sins. If you look to your left, those are the cages where we keep war criminals. Don't be surprised if you see a lot more US troops than you expected. Those guys are jerks."

Chris looked over at the cages, no bigger than the ones used to transport animals. The people inside were naked, weeping, their flesh charred. "Is this going to be like one of those near-death experience things?" Chris asked. "Afterwards, I go back to Earth and I write a book about what Hell is really like in order to encourage people to live better lives?"

The demon looked deadpan and sighed. "No this is going to be like one of those: you-died-for-real-and-got-sent-to-Hell things. But because you weren't *too* shitty a person you don't have to suffer. Instead you get given a job torturing the people who were really shitty."

"So then how good of a person do I have to be to go to Heaven?" Chris asked, running his fingers over the bumps on his forehead again.

"Stop fooling yourself kid," said the demon. "*No one* goes to Heaven. There are like five people up there. It's overrated anyway. Totally boring. They sit around drinking tea all day talking about how wonderful they were when they were alive. You really landed on one of the better outcomes as far as the human soul is concerned, trust me."

"But if not everyone goes to Heaven and not everyone goes to Hell, then where do all the rest go?"

"Do you really think that Earth, Heaven and Hell are the only three places souls can go? You have a lot to learn, Rocket Scientist." The demon pointed at one of the souls who was trying to claw its way out of a pit. "That one is trying to get away! Give it a good jab to remind it who's boss."

Chris readied his pitchfork but hesitated. "I don't know so much about this, I've never been much of a sadist."

The demon rolled his snake eyes before giving the crawling soul a sharp kick, sending it back into the pit where it was dragged down by its fellow sinners. The demon then took Chris by the shoulder and pointed down into another fiery pit. "See that guy?"

"Yeah," Chris replied.

"That is your primary school bully. He beat you up more times than I can count."

Chris looked a little closer and remembered. Sure enough, the man screaming in the pit was Tony Shepard. The person who made Chris's primary school career almost unbearable. "Son of a bitch," said Chris, before thrusting his pitchfork deep into the centre of Tony's chest. Tony shrieked before falling back and sliding off the prongs.

"I think you're more of a sadist than you realise," said the demon, checking off something else on his clipboard. "Keep it up and you may even make employee of the month."

Chris frowned at Tony writhing in the pit amongst all the other burning bodies.

"Don't overthink it," said the demon. "Tony went on to become a wife and child beater. Like I said, there isn't anyone here who doesn't deserve to be here. Being here is as much a part of their journey as yours. It's just a job, souls need to be punished so someone has to punish them. Supply and demand and all that."

Chris thought about his life. Memories were bubbling up to the surface of his mind. How many times had he suffered at the hands of others? Now he was the one who could dish out the suffering and the best part was, it was being dished out to people who actually deserved it. He took a good long look at his pitchfork and said, "I think I'm going to like it here."

17

BUDDHA'S DELIGHT

"You guys!" said Wren floating through the front door on her personal cloud of ethereal wonder. "The most wonderful thing happened to me on my inner city self-reflective walkabout this morning!"

Mark rolled his eyes from his spot on the couch where he was playing video games and Ian knew exactly what he was thinking, *here we go again.* They had been house mates with Wren for just over two years and were used to her strange habits. She was a self-proclaimed new age spiritualist, vegan and social justice activist. And would often enter the house from one of her walkabouts (which normal people would just call a walk) with some new-found deep spiritual knowledge only she had access to and felt a dire need to impart on anyone who would listen. They knew the drill by now and that was to just let Wren talk until she ran out of steam.

The house was covered in clusters of crystals and always smelled like incense but the rent was cheap so Ian and Mark were willing to put up with all the weird and wonderful things Wren got up to. She had at one time almost set fire to the dining room curtains with a smudge stick after which it was agreed that she would have to find an alternative method to perform her cleansings.

Today she was bustling with excitement and had in her hands several brown paper shopping bags as well as her usual handbag that looked like it had been made from the clothes of a thousand dead hippies. To Ian, as strange as Wren could be, she was also the most beautiful woman he had ever laid eyes on. And it wasn't just her looks, it was her spirit of freedom. Her long golden blonde hair always tumbled loose over her shoulders, her skin was like freshly whipped cream and her large cobalt eyes alive with a child-like wonder. Wren was always excited about something she had done, seen, planned to do or, in this case, discovered. Ian wasn't sure if he was in love with her or in love with how much she was in love with life. Ian got up to meet her at the door and help her with her shopping bags.

"I was on my way to grab my fat-free, dairy-free, sugar-free, locally sourced organic double soy raw cocoa digestive latte," she continued without prompt, "when my spirit guides told me to look up and there it was, the most amazing little esoteric store. It's the coolest place and best of all, it's owned by a real-life guru called Guru Bakavaada. He has such powerful energy. His whole vibe is totally out of this world. You guys have to come check it out with me. I'm going back with Robin tomorrow, Guru Bakavaada is going to do readings for us. You should come along!"

Ian nearly choked on his own saliva. "Wren, as much as I find all of this woo-woo shit you are into entertaining at times, that kind of thing really isn't my scene. Besides, I am sure you will post a million pictures of it to your Instagram so I can just check those out and it will be like I was really there."

"What's the matter Ian?" Mark teased from his seat on the couch. "Are you afraid the guru-man is going to tell you something you don't want to hear?"

"No," said Ian, shooting Mark a dirty look. "I just don't see why I should pay someone to talk bullshit in my ears when I can get it from my house mates for free."

"Oh, come on Ian!" Wren pleaded. "It will be fun, I will pay for you and then afterwards we can go for lunch. Maybe Guru will be able to give you some advice that will help you find a new job."

There was something about the look in Wren's big sapphire eyes that made Ian's heart beat a little faster. However the feeling in his heart didn't compensate for the jab of having Wren pity him so much.

"No amount of visits to a spiritual healer is going to get me a new job," said Ian. "At this point I feel like I am going to need a full on miracle and if not then I'd like to be struck down by lightning."

"Still no luck?" Wren asked looking doe-eyed and genuinely sympathetic.

"As unbelievable as it is, the web development market seems saturated," said Ian. "Every company I've applied to have either found someone else, uses a service that shits a website out for them, outsources the development work somewhere cheap or simply isn't looking. It's been months and all I've managed to get are a few freelance jobs."

Wren looked at Ian like she wanted to say something private but didn't feel comfortable in front of Mark. Ian couldn't stand having her look at him that way, like he was someone to be offered a hand out.

"I'm fine Wren," Ian said as gently as he possibly could. "I have money saved up and it will get me through until I find something more solid. I promise the rent will be on time."

"Oh please," said Wren, "I couldn't care less about the rent, nor would my parents. You have a lot on your plate, you pay a lot of your mom's bills and you've worked so hard to save that money for –"

Ian raised his palm and interrupted her. "I promise that I am perfectly fine and you don't have to worry. My mom is taken care of and so is the other thing. It will all be okay."

"Okay," Wren sighed. "But will you please come with tomorrow, I really think that Guru will be able to help you."

Ian hesitated for a moment before caving in. "Fine!" He threw his hands up in the air. "I will go with you to see your new witch doctor or whatever."

"Oooh," Wren squealed, throwing her arms around Ian. "This is going to be so much fun! You'll see!" The embrace didn't last quite as long as Ian would have liked. Wren always smelled good. Not like perfume or anything fancy, but like fresh linen being dried on a sunny day. She was always warm. Even in the middle of the coldest winter nights her hands and smile radiated a cosy warmth Ian could never get enough of. Ian watched her disappear to her bedroom with her shopping bags.

"Dude," Mark said, "I have seen snails nailed to the floor that move faster than you do with that girl."

"What are you talking about?" Ian asked, whipping his head away from Wren's bedroom door toward Mark.

Mark threw his head back in laughter. "It's as clear as day

to everyone else that you are into Little Miss Magic but you don't want to admit it."

Ian scoffed, "Whatever. I…I'm…Whatever. Shut up!"

"Just admit it! Robin seems to think that she is into you too."

"What the hell would Robin know about it?" Ian said, his cheeks growing hot.

"Do you live under a rock?" Mark asked, looking at Ian like he was from another planet. "Robin is her gay bestie. She tells that guy everything, he might as well be her living, breathing journal."

"What did Robin say to you?" Ian tried to sound as nonchalant as possible.

"Oh so you do like Wren!" Mark exclaimed, slamming the gaming control into a couch cushion.

"I don't!" Ian said as forcefully as he could, trying to maintain a tone that would not be overheard by Wren.

"Then why do you care about knowing what she told Robin?" Mark asked as his lips formed an impish smile.

"You know what? I don't care." Ian said, throwing his hands up and walking toward his room.

"Yeah, sure you don't," Mark called after him. "That is why you are gonna let some Wizard of Oz wannabe look at your palm tomorrow and tell you how many kids you'll have, hopefully with Wren! I know you don't believe in any of that shit! That's how I know you are only going because she asked you to."

"I have work to do," said Ian, ending the conversation and walking into his bedroom.

"I think I'll tag a long tomorrow," said Mark. "I don't want to miss it when the Wizard gives you courage or a brain or balls or whatever the fuck you're missing that's stopping you from making a move!"

Ian closed his bedroom door. He was annoyed with himself for being so transparent. Mark was right of course. Everything about Wren fascinated Ian. He could look at her for hours – he didn't because that would be creepy but he *could*. He loved the way she would bring a cup of tea to her full lips, upon which she always wore the same ruby lipstick. He liked the way she would gently tap her temple with her ring finger when she was concentrating and the way she would bite her bottom lip just a little when she was reading or watching something thrilling. He like the way droplets of sweat would collect on her face when she came back from a run, and how those same droplets would fall down her long smooth neck and disappear into the space between her beautiful plump breasts.

Not that it made any difference, he had never and probably would never tell her how he felt about her. There was too much getting in his way. Sure, both Ian and Wren were single but Ian didn't think of himself as the type of guy who would normally pick Wren up for a date.

Ian always thought if anyone in the house had a shot at it with Wren it would be Mark, he was the one with the bulging muscles and the love of sports cars and whiskey. Mark was similar to the men Wren would normally go for. But in the two years they had been living together Mark had never shown the slightest bit of interest in her.

These days Ian liked to keep an especially healthy distance from the idea of him and Wren as a couple. If it worked out then great but if it didn't and she rejected him then it would make the living situation awkward for all three of them. Ian wasn't in the position to be looking for a new place to live, especially not without a steady job. That was the other problem, why would someone as wonderful and beautiful as Wren go for a man on the verge of becoming a bum?

The house was owned by Wren's parents. They were wealthy property developers and charged both Ian and Mark rent way below the market norm. Ian thought that it was because Wren's parent's liked the idea of having two men in the house to watch out for her, which Mark and Ian did. If something broke, he and Mark fixed it. If something needed to be installed, he and Mark would do it. If anyone gave Wren trouble, well Mark did knock a guy out once for smacking Wren on the ass when they were out at a club one night. Ian was better at handling admin for Wren, like negotiating better internet service provider prices and showing her how to get the most out of her tax returns.

Ian fell into the chair at his desk and his eyes fell to the framed photo of him, his mom and dad. It was one of those super cheesy photos from a photoshoot you could have done at the mall. Ian smiled at the photo and opened his desk drawer. Inside was a brown cardboard box marked: S Barber.

"Hey dad," said Ian to the box before gently picking it up and placing it on the desk. "Long time no see. I've been super busy the last couple of months but I'm sure things will calm down soon and then you, Mom and I can finally take that trip that you always wanted."

Ian fired up his computer and the monitor glowed to life. He moved the cursor to a folder on his desk top titled: *Aurora Borealis*, clicked it and the holiday plans leaped onto the screen. "See dad, I've got it all planned out." Ian scrolled through the images of snow-covered Sweden and the northern sky lit up by gigantic glowing auroras. "I've been saving up for a long time now and I almost have enough to take all three of us. We'll go soon and it will be just like it used to be – you, Mom and me."

Ian put his father back inside the desk drawer, closed the holiday folder on his computer and opened the folder titled: *Budget*. A spreadsheet opened and Ian didn't like the look of it. Not having a job was devouring his savings. Between the repayments on his student loans, the bills that he took care of for his mom and his monthly living expenses, it wouldn't be long before there was nothing left. He lowered his head, closed his eyes and sighed. He couldn't give up. He had to keep trying to find a new job while at the same time acquiring freelance work to help stop him dipping too far into the Sweden trip money.

Ian's parents were in their early forties when his mom fell pregnant with him. Growing up with parent's who were a little older had its pros and cons, one of the cons being that they die when their children are still young. This has been that case with Ian's father, who had died from a heart attack at 61 when Ian was only 18. What his parents didn't know about finances they made up for in love. This wasn't always helpful, especially when it came to very pricey things like a university education. Ian and his mother had managed until Ian was able to support himself and take care of her larger monthly expenses that her meagre pension would never be able to cover. Evangeline Barber knew all about the Sweden trip. She was as invested in it as Ian was and they had agreed to say goodbye to Ian's father under the Northern Lights not long after he passed away. Evangeline was however not privy to the fact that her son had been out of work for the past four months.

Ian pushed the thoughts of his mother, the Sweden trip and Wren from his mind by diving into some freelance work he had to get done. Ian liked coding, it wasn't complicated like people were. You wrote it and if it was correct it worked, if it wasn't correct you had to go in and figure out what you did wrong. Code didn't ask a million job application questions, or play games with him like Mark, or remain painfully out of reach like Wren.

With a click of his mouse the lines of code flashed up on his monitor and Ian's fingers began to fly over his keyboard. He typed out line after line of HTML and CSS until he wasn't annoyed with Mark or frustrated about Wren anymore. He coded and coded until he was too tired to be stressed out about the lack of work and the trip to Sweden he desperately wanted to take his mother on. When he looked at the time in the bottom right side of his monitor it was well after one in the morning. Fatigue fall over him like a heavy blanket. He needed to get some rest before the big day with Guru Bullshit. Ian pulled his glasses off and crawled into bed. When he closed his eyes he could still see the lines of code burned into his retina from hours at the computer. They all read with the same commands:

<h1>Wren</h1><a href= "Wren"</a> Wren Wren....

Ω

"Well?" Wren asked beaming with giddy excitement. "What do you think?"

"I think it looks like every other place you buy your incense," said Mark with a raised eyebrow.

They were standing in the parking lot of the strip mall where Wren liked to get her coffee – which was now also home to *Buddha's Delight*, where the store owner would soon be telling their alleged fortunes. The smell of incense was already burning a hole through Ian's sinuses.

The store's name hung in massive copper letters above the entrance and the large windows, giving passers-by a clear view of all the trinkets and treasures they could purchase on their path to enlightenment.

"This is going to be so cool!" Wren said grabbing Ian's hand and towing him toward the store. Her touch was warm as ever and Ian tried not to panic. If he panicked his palms would get sweaty and Wren's had would slip away from his like a live fish.

A bamboo wind chime gave a hollow rattle as Wren pushed the door open. Ian's senses were immediately assaulted by sights, sounds and smells. The trickle of water features over the soft humming of Tibetan monks wandered over his ear drums and the smell of burning incense was now so strong it should have been illegal. The walls on the inside had been painted with Hindu and Buddhist deities in a street art style that made the very timid religions seem edgy and hip, like Buddha had decided to appeal to a fresh new market. He wasn't a regular Buddha, he was a cool Buddha. Ian and Wren were shortly followed inside by Mark and Robin.

A man, who was unmistakably the Guru and owner Wren had told them about appeared from behind a curtain at the other end of the store. The man wore an acid green turban with a large purple gemstone broach pinned to his right shoulder. His brown eyes were framed by eyeliner that looked like it had been applied with a hammer. His crowning glory was his long black beard that flowed down his front and was braided with green ribbons. At the end of each green and black braid hung a little bell which jingled as he walked towards them. He was dressed in a black and purple robe draped over his skeletal frame.

"Welcome!" he greeted opening his arms. There was not a finger that didn't have at least three rings on it set with a stone or symbol of some sort. A wide smile made its way out from behind the beard, displaying a mouthful of narrow yellow teeth. As the man stepped closer, Ian noticed that he was barefoot and his toenails were in desperate need of a clean and clip.

"Are you fucking kidding me?" Ian asked Wren. "The guy looks like a homeless acid trip."

"Be nice," Wren whispered through gritted teeth before approaching the man and giving him a hug. "Guru Bakavaada, Namaste! These are my friends," she said pointing at them with an open palm, "Robin, Mark and Ian."

Guru nodded his turban-clad head at the group, turned back to Wren and took her hands in his, "When you light a lamp for someone else," he said, "it will also brighten your path." His voice was pleasantly deep and smooth and had a soothing quality that even Ian had to admit had a certain magnetism about it.

"He is so wise," Wren whispered to Ian.

"Oh you're white," said Mark.

"What the hell, Mark!" yelled Robin, giving Mark a slap on the arm. "You can't say things like that."

Mark didn't even flinch, "I'm sorry," he said. "From Wren's description of you, I thought you would be Indian or something. And also a little older."

"Not to worry my new friend," said the man. "All that we are is a result of what we have thought. The mind is everything. What we think we become."

Mark shot Ian a confused look. Ian looked away, but was glad he was not alone in thinking that this man was a nutcase.

The Guru motioned for them to follow him and he led them passed a tall bookshelf. On the other side was a coffee table surrounded by eight small bean bags and a few foot stools. On the coffee table, a tea set had been arranged and steam was wafting from the spout of the tea pot.

"Please," the Guru said, "enjoy some jasmine tea while I take whoever wants to go first for their reading."

"Ian wants to go first," said Mark before anyone else had a chance to speak. "He's really excited. Aren't you Ian?"

Ian, not wanting to look miserable in front of Wren, didn't say what he really wanted to Mark. Instead he just gave a stupid smile and followed the Guru. He was led through heavy violet curtains to the back of the shop that gave an entirely different impression than the front. The small round candlelit room held every cliché from every movie about the supernatural Ian had ever seen. The walls were curtains of heavy red fabric and shelves everywhere hosted the random flotsam and jetsam one would expect to see in a fortune teller's chamber. Crystal balls in various shades and sizes (one even looked like a skull), a Ouija board, a box full of smudge sticks and different decks of tarot were among the few things that Ian could identify. More incense burned off to the side, the smell was starting to give him a headache.

"Wow this place is camp," he said without thinking. His hand flew to his mouth to stop anything else rude that may have wanted to slip out.

"Don't worry," said the Guru, "I am not offended. Better to be slapped with the truth than kissed with a lie. This room has a way of bringing one's real thoughts and feelings to the surface."

"You're talking about the place like it's some ancient place of power," said Ian. "Two months ago this was a store that sold CBD products and a few months before that it was a Thai restaurant that got shut down for health and safety violations."

"It is not where we are that matters," said the Guru, from under the green turban, "but what we bring with us."

"Oh my god," Ian shot back, "no wonder Wren is bananas for you. You sound like a Deepak Chopra audio book."

"Please take a seat," he said. "Have you ever had a reading done for you before?"

Ian pulled up one of the heavy wooden chairs and sat down on its lumpy red velvet cushion. "No," he answered. "I've never been stupid enough to have it done before."

"Love can hold a mysterious power over people," the Guru said.

Ian wanted to ask him what he meant by that but he didn't get a chance before the Guru started speaking again.

"The readings I give are a little unconventional, not that you would know, having never been for one. But it is a disclaimer I offer all my visitors." The Guru scanned over Ian with his dark soot-smudged eyes and a chill rippled down Ian's spine.

The Guru then took out a deck of tarot cards, passed them to Ian and said, "Shuffle them."

Ian did as he was told but didn't like the way the cards felt in his hands. They were dry and crusty against his fingers. He handed them back after only shuffling a little. As soon as the cards touched the Guru's hand all the candles in the room dimmed and the temperature plummeted. The Guru pulled three cards from the top of the deck and laid them out in front of Ian, facedown.

"These three cards represent your past, present and future," said the Guru. He turned the first one over to reveal the image of a tree with a thick trunk and healthy green leaves reaching up towards a golden sun. "This card is the Sacred Tree," said the Guru. "It tells us that your roots run deep and you are not easily shaken. You have been growing towards a goal for a long time and you are almost at the point of achieving it."

He then flipped over the second card that had a picture of some kind of Indian elephant god on it. Ian had to turn his head to get a better look at it because this card had come out upside down.

"Interesting," said the Guru. This card is Ganesha, he is known as the remover of obstacles but he is upside down. This tells us that you have come to an obstacle, blockage or obstruction. Something or someone is stopping you from achieving your goal. Not to worry though, most times when people get this card, it means that they are only standing in their own way."

The Guru then flipped the third and final card over, this

one depicted an old man with a knife raised above his head, poised to stab younger man who was laid on an altar. "Father Abraham," said the Guru. "He is a symbol of sacrifice. This tells us that in order to remove your obstacle and achieve the goal you're working towards, you will need to be willing to make a great sacrifice."

"So to put everything into perspective, you were thriving but now something is in your way. Does this remind you of anything in your life? Perhaps it has something to do with your friend who brought you here. You desire her, and I don't need to be able to read the future to tell me that, it is as plain as the glasses on your face."

Ian didn't say anything. He just sat there with the chill settled in his spine. Wren must have mentioned something to this guy about the trip to spread his father's ashes and Ian's lack of a 9 to 5. He squirmed in his seat with the strong desire to leave.

"Not to worry, new friend," said the man. "Guru Bakavaada is here to help you!"

Before Ian could object the Guru pulled out some paper and box of coloured chalk from under the table and started sketching frantically. Ian wanted to tell him to stop but the man had fallen into a trance. His eyes had rolled back in their sockets and he was drawing like he was no longer in control of his body but rather a puppet for something else. This went on for several minutes with the puppet-guru putting one colour of chalk down and picking up another to draw with. It finally came to an end with the Guru sitting up, taking a deep breath and his eyes rolling back where they belonged.

"Quite the performance," Ian said. "You should drool a

little next time, it would really tie the whole thing together. Are you done?"

"Yes," said the Guru smiling his yellow smile and sliding the chalk drawing across the table to Ian. "That is your spirit guide. He will watch over you and make sure that you get what you need in order to overcome your obstacles."

Ian picked the drawing up, it looked like a cross between a Picasso and the kind of drawing that was used to help people identify criminals. "Umm, thanks I guess," he said. "Are we done? Can I go?"

"The reading is complete," said the Guru bringing his chalk dusted palms together and leaning forward in a small bow. He stood up and held back the curtain while Ian stepped through.

Ian's eyes had to adjust to the bright light in the main part of the store.

"Can I interest you in some tools that will help you remove your personal obstacles?" asked the Guru as he picked up a few items. "A Ganesha statue to help remove obstacles, some amethyst crystals for energy healing, incense for cleansing and meditation and a dried lavender pouch to attract harmony and romance."

"No thanks," said Ian.

"How was it?" Wren asked, standing up from her beanbag at the coffee table. Her eyes were bright and full of excitement.

"I need some fresh air," said Ian. "I'm going to wait outside." He walked out of the store, bursting through the invisible chanting cloud of incense smoke and nonsense. On his way to the car he threw the chalk drawing in one of the parking lot trash cans.

Ω

"I THOUGHT he was incredibly insightful and helpful," said Wren from behind her mound of Buddha's Delight purchases. She was unpacking and sorting her new collection of useless mystic knickknacks on the lounge floor before adding them to her old collection of useless mystic knickknacks. The group had come home after their readings and were now waiting for the lunch they had ordered. "He even gave me this cool necklace for free," she said leaning in closer showing Ian the clay charm hanging around her neck – a disc with a complex symbol made up of lines, squiggles and arrows carved into it. "He told me that it is an ancient sigil for abundance."

"For the abundance of money you spent there today," said Ian from his spot on the couch, "I would hope he gave you something for free."

"That man is bizarre," said Robin. "He knew so much about me. You should've had a reading Mark, it was very insightful."

"No thanks," said Mark crossing his arms, I was there purely for the entertainment value." He shot a smile in Ian's direction. Ian looked down at the floor.

"That tarot deck he used was interesting too," said Wren. "I've never seen one like that before."

Ian turned his gaze to Wren's bookshelf that held her personal collection of tarot card decks and counted twelve that he could see.

"It was pretty cool," said Robin.

"What about you Ian?" Wren asked. "What did you think

of your reading? Did he offer any advice for your predicament?"

"I don't need crystals and incense to solve my problems, Wren," Ian said trying to sound kind. "I need work." Ian could feel his face turning red with frustration at himself. He should have spent the time he wasted in that ridiculous shop applying for jobs.

The electric grind of the doorbell rang through the house. "That's the food. I'll get it." Ian got up and walked towards the door, grateful for the easy escape from the conversation. He accepted the bags of food from the delivery man and took them into the kitchen where Wren was waiting for him.

She watched him while he unpacked the polystyrene containers of Chinese food. He nearly jumped when she put her hand on top of his. Her touch was warm as always and his tight shoulders relaxed into jelly.

"It'll be okay," she said in a genuine attempt to comfort him. "You just need to have a little faith."

Ian slammed one of the food containers down on the counter harder than he meant to, sending sweet and sour pork oozing out the sides.

"Faith isn't going to help me get my mom to Sweden to scatter my dad's ashes, Wren." He said fighting back at the hot tears charging on his eyes. "I'm scared if I keep putting the trip off my mom is going to die before we get to go. I don't want to be left with two boxes of ashes and no closure. I have to make this happen, my dad used to talk about this trip all the time before he got sick. I need to do this for my mom and I need to do this for myself."

Wren didn't say anything, instead she stepped closer and wrapped her arms around Ian. His arms then found their way around her like it was something he had been doing forever. She squeezed him tightly, almost knocking his glasses from his face, and pressed her cheek against his chest. They stood that way until Ian felt strong enough to carry on.

Ω

IT STARTED WITH A LIGHT COUGH. A week later Wren was taken to the hospital in an ambulance. Another week passed and the doctors still had no idea what was wrong with her. In the space of 14 days Wren had gone from being the glowing picture of health to corpselike.

At the hospital Ian took her hand and for the first time in the two years he had known her, her skin was not just cold but icy. Ian didn't recognise the woman lying in the bed. All the colour had been drained from Wren's skin, leaving her grey and clammy. The fullness of her face had abandoned her, making her look haggard with her cheek bones protruding like spikes. Her lips had blistered and chapped and when her eyes were open, which wasn't often, the sparkling blue they once were was now a sad washed out grey. Her pleasant scent of sunshine had disappeared, in its place was a loamy and sour intruder of a smell. She was still wearing the necklace she got from the Guru, it lay loose around her neck while the clay amulet attached to it sat in the pale bony hollow of her neck.

Ian looked down at Wren with a creased brow. Everything he loved about her was slowly flickering out of existence. Seeing her lying in the bed like that reminded Ian of how his father had also laid in a hospital bed, fading away until there was nothing left of him but a box of grey ash in Ian's desk drawer.

Ian gave her icicle fingers a gentle squeeze and turned to leave. Her parents were on their way in and Ian wanted to give them some privacy. In the hallway Mark and Robin were waiting for him next to a half empty vending machine.

"Hey buddy," said Mark, throwing his arm around Ian. "How are you holding up?"

"It's hard on everyone," said Ian.

"I can't believe they don't know what is wrong with her," said Robin. He looked tired, Ian had watched the dark circles around his eyes grow wider and puffier every day for the past two weeks. "They've run every test under the sun and tried all the medicine they can think of. Wren's mom told me if they can't figure it out soon Wren isn't going…" Robin couldn't finish his sentence. Instead he swallowed hard and wiped tears away from his eyes. Mark then let go of Ian and embraced Robin as the three of them walked out of the hospital.

They climbed into Mark's Audi and sat in silence. Mark didn't even turn the heater on, despite the early winter chill that had gripped the night air.

"I hate feeling helpless like this," Ian said. "It was the same with my dad."

Mark patted Ian's shoulder before turning the car on and driving out of the parking lot. "If it were one of us in there do you know what Wren would say?"

"That we should have faith," Robin said, popping his head between the driver and passenger seats.

"Exactly," said Mark. "She wouldn't lose faith in us so we can't lose faith in her."

Ian turned his head and looked out the window. Mark was right, Wren wouldn't give up faith if the situation was the other way around. Even if it meant that having faith didn't make any sense. His mind wondered as he looked out the window at the houses and dim street lights rolling past.

Maybe if modern medicine was failing Wren, her problem wasn't medical. What if the problem was…no. As soon as the thought bubbled to the surface of his mind, Ian cringed at his own desperation. But there was nothing he could do about it, the thought was there now. What if Wren's health problems were somehow spiritual? He thought of Wren in the hospital bed, her body turning grey and lifeless. At this point he was willing to try anything. She would for him.

Ω

IAN'S FINGERS hovered over his keyboard. He didn't even know where to start looking for answers and felt stupid for even trying. He let his determination to help Wren drive his fingers forward and typed *spiritual illness* into the search engine. Ian hit enter and was sent down a black hole of search results. One of the most memorable results was for a store that sold crystal eggs you are supposed to stick in a place crystal eggs should never be stuck. He scrolled and clicked and read, jumping from website to website promoting healing teas, necklaces, statues and candles.

Maybe he was looking in the wrong place – he didn't know what he was doing. He should be speaking to that Guru Wren loves so much. Ian's eyes then fell on a search result he hadn't clicked on yet. It read:

Magical solutions for magical problems | Cobblestone Witches Three

No hex we can't vex. No curse we can't reverse. Mistresses of magic, purveyors of potions, tellers of the tarot and astrology. Cobblestone witches three, bring you magical solutions to all your problems, mundane or supernatural. Let us help you kick demonic possession out the back door while inviting love in through the front door. With over three hundred years combined esoteric experience Circe, Mortencia and Euphoria Cobblestone promise powerful results.

Ian clicked on the result and was taken to a website that, in his professional opinion, could have used some work. It was outdated and slow. When the page did eventually load, a pop up appeared that read:

The witch is in! **Click here** to start a FREE video chat.

"I'm losing my mind," he said to himself as he hovered the cursor over the pop up. "Virus or porn, let's see what you really are." He clicked and live video feed of the face of an old woman appeared on the monitor. "Oh shit, it's porn!" Ian yelled and rushed to click away.

"Excuse you young man," said the old woman. "Firstly, it's called erotic art and secondly this is not it, though I am flattered you would think that."

Ian let go of his mouse. "Are you the witch?"

"Well I'm definitely not a priest," she said before letting out a cackle. "Circe Cobblestone at your service. How can I help you?" Her green eyes were warm and welcoming, and her face, while ancient, was friendly. A lot of the screen was filled with her wild white curls that ran thick and long from the top of her head.

"I'm Ian," he said. "I don't believe in any of this stuff but I have a friend who does and she's really sick. Dying actually. I was looking for something that could help her."

The witch frowned, an expression that did not seem natural for her otherwise cheerful old face. "Oh dear child," she said. "I'm sorry but there is nothing that we can do about the natural progression of life. When it's your time to go, it's your time."

"But that's the thing," said Ian. "I don't think what's happening to her is natural. That's how I found you. The doctors have been testing her for a two weeks and they can't figure out what is wrong with her."

The old woman raised a grey eyebrow before reaching for a digital tablet and placing a pair of small round wire-rimmed spectacles on her nose. She started typing and scrolling on the tablet. "Can you describe her symptoms to me please?"

"She went from being really healthy to really weak in the space of a few days. She had a cough and it went downhill from there. She's wasting away and her skin has gone a funny grey colour and even her eyes don't look the same as they used to. She is cold, cold like ice. She was never cold before, always warm."

Circe continued to scroll on her tablet. "Tell me," she said, "how would you have described this friend before she got ill? Was she full of life? Beautiful?"

"Being around her was like standing in sunshine," said Ian.

"I see," she said. "Has she met anyone new lately or made any recent changes in her life?"

Ian thought for a moment. "The Guru," he said thinking out loud.

"What did you say?" said the witch, her head shooting up from her tablet, her eyes wide.

"She met some Guru like two weeks ago, we all went to him for a reading. He owns a store not far from where we live that sells all sorts of spiritual stuff."

The old woman put the tablet down. "Did your friend by anything from this gentleman?

Ian scoffed. "Only about the whole damn store. What does it matter?"

"It matters because what you are dealing with, my dear boy, is a parasite. A leach that siphons off the life force of other creatures through dark magic."

Ian wanted to roll his eyes, but didn't. "Let's say I believe what you are saying, what should I do?"

"To start with, you need to sever all the connections he has to your friend. Burn everything she bought from that creature," said Circe.

"That might take a while," said Ian thinking off all the things Wren had bought, "but it's not impossible. Then what?"

"You need to disrupt the flow of the siphon by getting the leach to take something from you."

"What could he possibly want that I have?" Ian asked.

"It will have to be something of great importance to catch his fancy," said Circe. "There is powerful magic in sacrifice. He won't be interested in the physical thing, he'll want the magical energy that will come with the exchange. He will be able to feed off it and when he is done, he will have to let go of the connection to your friend. Provided you destroy everything he sold her."

Ian racked his brain but there was only one thing he could think of. "I've been saving money to do something important with. Would that work?"

"I'm afraid he will be interested in something more precious than money," said Circe looking at Ian like he already knew exactly what the Guru would really be interested in.

"He'd want my dad's ashes," Ian stared blankly passed the monitor.

Circe's old eyes widened. "Human remains have incredibly powerful magical properties. That combined with the magical energy he would get from the sacrifice would be immense. There is no way he'll be able to resist. Ian, do you have anything black?"

"Um," said Ian looking around his desk. "I have this black pen." He picked it up and held it in front of the webcam.

"That will work well," said Circe. "Keep it there and be quiet for a moment." The witch closed her eyes and the temperature in Ian's room began to rise. The bedroom light and his computer monitor flickered.

"What the –"

"Ssshhh," the witch hushed and a gust of wind blew through the room then died down as quickly as it arrived. The light stopped flickering and the woman opened her eyes again. "As soon as he takes the ashes from you, I want you to stab him with that pen. That in combination with the magical energy generated by the sacrifice should be enough to take care of your problem. Now go save your friend and get that beast out of your lives for good."

"I'll do it," said Ian, trying to convince himself that any of this was sane.

"There is just one last thing you need to know," said Circe. "When you do this your father's ashes will be destroyed in the process."

Ian looked down at the draw that held all that was left of his father. "I understand," he said. "Thank you for your help."

"You're welcome," said Circe. "And when all of this is over, send me an email. I'm in the market for a new web developer. My website is atrocious."

"How did you know I'm a –"

"Good luck my child," she interrupted. "Be strong and make haste! Your friend doesn't have much time!"

The video window went blank and Ian jumped from his chair. As crazy as it sounded, he knew what he had to do.

Ω

HE BURNT IT ALL.

As soon as the call with the witch ended, Ian ran around the house like a mad man gathering up everything he was sure Wren had bought from the Guru. He piled it up in the backyard, poured lighter fluid on it and sent it up in flames.

It wasn't until the fire was burning high that he remembered Wren was still wearing the necklace she'd been gifted by the Guru. It too had to go. He'd have to make a pit stop at the hospital on his way to Buddha's Delight. He ran back inside the house, grabbed his car keys, his father's ashes, the pen from his desk and bolted for the front door. As his fingers touched the door handle Mark cried out.

"What that fuck, Ian! Why is the backyard on fire?"

Ian turned, Robin was standing behind Mark looking shaken. "I don't have time to explain. It's to help Wren. Just…" he struggled for something to say to explain his insane behaviour as he opened the door, "have faith!"

As he sped down the road Ian glanced at the clock on the dashboard. Visiting hours would be over soon, he had to hurry. His car flew into a parking spot and he jumped out, not knowing if he even closed the car door behind him. He scuttled through the passages of the hospital and jogged up the stairs, taking care not to attract too much attention, until he reached the floor Wren's room was on. He turned the corner into her room and froze in his tracks.

"Mom," he said. "What are you doing here?"

Ian's mother turned away from Wren's bedside at the sound of Ian's voice. "Ian, what's the matter?" She walked to Ian and pressed the back of her hand to his forehead. "You're as white as a ghost and sweating buckets."

"I don't have time," he said. "I need to help Wren." He walked around his mother and leaned over Wren. She looked even worse than when he had seen her a few hours before. He reached for the necklace and, as gently as he could, snapped it away.

"You told me Wren was sick so I came to see her," said Evangeline with her forehead creased in worry. "Her parents are still here, they just went to get something to eat."

"I have to go, Mom," Ian said as he was on his way out. An ache in his heart stopped him from taking another step. "Mom."

"Yes dear?" said Evangeline

"You know I love you right? And that I wouldn't do anything to hurt you."

"Ian, you have me very worried, I need you to tell me –"

"Just answer me, Mom!"

"Yes, Ian! I know, and I love you too."

"I have to go," he slipped out of the room, unable to turn back and look at his mother's face.

Ω

THE DRIVE to the strip mall was a frantic blur. The parking lot was deserted under the cover of the cloudless night sky with nothing but the street lamps and the moon to light Ian's way. His hands shook and fumbled at the latch to open the cubbyhole from which he retrieved his father's ashes and the black pen.

Outside the shop the Guru was waiting in the shadows but he was different than the last time Ian had seen him. He wore the same green turban and robes but his smile of warm welcome had been replaced with a grimace.

As Ian climbed out the car and approached, the Guru called out to him.

"You have been messing with my plans," he hissed. Behind his cracked lips Ian saw an oily forked tongue brush over his yellowing teeth. Ian walked on despite his sweating palms, clobbering heart and churning stomach.

"I want you to leave Wren alone!" Ian yelled before pulling the necklace from his pocket, throwing it to the ground and stomping on it with the heel of his shoe. The clay amulet cracked and the Guru flinched. "I have something to offer you in exchange." He held up the box of ashes.

The Guru's eyes focused on the box and then widened with delight. "That will do nicely." He said stepping closer to

Ian. He moved different to before. His steps were no longer light and breezy, now more like a predator stalking its prey.

"If I give you these," said Ian shaking all he had left of his father, "you need to promise me that Wren will be alright."

"Very well." The Guru drew closer and reached out with his bony hand, his black eyes locked on the box.

Ian stepped closer and extended his own hand, they were almost close enough to make contact but Ian had to make sure he was close enough to the Guru to stab him with the pen. The Guru's long fingernails scraped the side of the box when both he and Ian were drenched in the light from the headlights of a car. Ian tightened his grip on the box and jerked his head around towards the car. The lights went out and three of the car's doors opened. His mother emerged from the driver's seat followed by Mark from the passenger's side and Robin from the back.

"A trick!" spat the Guru, his hateful black eyes driving daggers toward Ian. The wind picked up from nowhere and began to howl through the parking lot.

"Ian!" his mother yelled, "What are you doing?"

"I'm so sorry, Mom!" Ian yelled back before taking a step closer to the Guru. "It's no trick," said Ian, pushing the box into the Guru's clawed hand. "Just take them and leave Wren alone!" The wind picked up speed, making the bells at the end of the Guru's beard jingle. Evangeline's screams were drowned out by the violent wind.

The Guru's other hand grabbed Ian's shoulder and the sharp nails dug into his flesh. Ian screamed as a vacuum formed over his body, pulling at him from every direction. The lamplights flickered and the Guru's eyes began to glow green. Ian reached into his back pocket for the pen and gripped it tightly in his fist. Lunging forward, he drove the pen with all the force he could muster into the Guru's chest.

The Guru's talons dislodged from Ian's shoulder and the man fell back. He held Ian's father in one hand while the other reached for the pen. He ripped the pen from his flesh and black goo oozed from the wound, staining his robes. Green embers began to glow all over his body making him look like he was under attack by an armada of glow worms. The wind fanned the embers and they burst into great emerald flames.

The Guru fell to his knees. "You wicked boy!" He shrieked. "What have you done to me? A thousand curses upon you until the end of time!" The Guru was then engulfed in the flames and the box of ashes with him, his cries of agony carried on the wind.

A second green fire had sprung up inside the shop and a whirlwind of flame burst through the windows. Within seconds the store became an inferno.

The Guru continued to screech as he flailed back and forth until both he and the store exploded, throwing Ian from his feet and hurling him backwards. He landed on his back, the cold asphalt of the parking lot scraping at his skin. His mother, Mark and Robin rushed to his side.

"Ian!" his mother yelled grabbing his arms. "Oh my God! Are you alright?"

Ian groaned and kept his eyes closed as he sat up. "I'm fine," he said, rubbing the back of his head and touching a warm wet spot. The back of his arms burned where the asphalt had grated his skin open. "I'm so sorry mom," he cried into his mother's shoulder. "I had to give him Dad's ashes. He was killing Wren. I had to do something."

"It's alright," said Evangeline holding him closer. "I'm just glad you are okay. We need to get you to the hospital."

"It's not alright," he sobbed. "Now we can never say goodbye to Dad the way we were supposed to."

"I'm not so sure about that," said Mark from behind them.

Ian looked up from his mom's shoulder and opened his eyes. The parking lot was bathed in a soft green light and Mark was pointing towards the sky. Both Ian, Robin and Evangeline looked up, their mouths fell open.

The sky had come alive with immense dancing ribbons of green light. The light twisted and refracted, changing colour from green to pink to purple and blue then back to green.

Evangeline gasped as her hand flew over her mouth and tears welled up in her eyes. Ian rose to his feet, then helped her up and held her close.

"What is it?" Robin asked, awe struck.

Ian smiled through his tears and without looking away replied, "It's an aurora.

ACKNOWLEDGEMENTS

It took a village to get the finished product that is this book into your hands. I want to use this page to say thank you to that village.

To my family, thank you for being a constant source of inspiration and support. I know I talk a lot, thank you for always listening.

Berno, it's not easy having me for a partner. Thank you for the endless cups of coffee, delicious meals and support. I could not have asked for a better person to share my life and my work with. Ek is baie lief vir jou!

My brother and story editor, Ryan Ferguson. The only thing more difficult than giving someone a first draft to read, is reading someone's first draft. Thank you for the endless phone calls spent discussing stories, characters, plot points and cover options. Without your input this book would be considerably shittier.

My copy editor, Catherine Bower, thank you for being a great editor and an even greater friend. Without your valuable input this book would be riddled with mistakes.

Special thanks to Dr. Arjen Barnard for answering my gross, morbid and weird questions.

Special thanks to my father, Grant Ferguson, for buying me all those weird children's books when I was growing up. They really helped refine my taste in stories all the way into adulthood.

My advanced copy readers; Berno, Lauren, Aimee, Nathan and Grant, thank you so much for helping me build enough confidence to put my work out into the world.

ABOUT THE AUTHOR

Michael Ferguson leads a quiet life. He spends most of his free time in his purple bathrobe writing stories, painting pictures and eating chocolate. When he is not doing those things he is making a fool of himself on several different social media platforms, including but not limited to Instagram and YouTube. He is a chatterbox and attention whore of the highest order. Go say hello to him on one of the aforementioned social media platforms, he will like that.

When he is dead, he would like the following quote to be shared by people in memory of him:

"Do not speak quietly about the things that set your soul on fire, shout them so that even the uninterested will have no choice but to hear you."- Michael-John "Kwezi" Ferguson

Just make sure the quote is shared under a picture of Matt Bomer. This will trick people into thinking Michael was vastly more attractive than he really was.